SOAR

The Ultimate Soul Mate Journey

JOHN CICERO

authorHOUSE®

AuthorHouse™
1663 Liberty Drive
Bloomington, IN 47403
www.authorhouse.com
Phone: 833-262-8899

Published by AuthorHouse 10/11/2022

ISBN: 978-1-6655-7328-3 (sc)
ISBN: 978-1-6655-7329-0 (hc)
ISBN: 978-1-6655-7327-6 (e)

For Debra, My Soulmate

Contents

Acknowledgments

Brittani, Mike, Luke, Joey, Alicia and Anthony,

Soar is one of those stories I just had to write. It's ultimately my very special and unique love letter to Mom, who will always be my eternal soulmate.

The overarching theme of *Soar* may be difficult at times, but it's one I feel is important to better understand, embrace, and ideally use as an instrument to inspire and provide comfort for all who have faced life-altering events in their lives.

Our family has been through its share of life-altering events the last few years, and I could not be prouder as you all continue to amaze me with your strength, faith, and perseverance. Always, stay the course in your faithful ways, and remain secure in your family roots.

To our family and dear friends, you truly provide that dependable and comforting support to our rock-solid foundation. We cannot thank you enough for your ongoing love and encouragement.

Debra, you will always and forever be my world and my everything. Your ever-present strength and most special spirit inspire us every day. I love you beyond words!

As always, a very special thank you and acknowledgment to DeAnn Bartram for her amazing support, motivation, and editing of *Soar, the Ultimate Soulmate Journey*.

Chapter One

The Morning Everything Changed

This is a story about a man named Jack and a woman named Dolly, who fell in love and had three amazing children, a cherished life together, and one dog. But fate's ultimate plan, and clearly not one of their own, came far too early for one of them.

It may seem uncharacteristic to begin a story with the end, but this story will show that the perceived end is actually the most beautiful beginning any of us could possibly imagine. In fact, this end is the ultimate destination and journey we will all take when our time is ripe.

Jack Mandisa had imagined this passage for quite some time, especially in those amazing seconds immediately after Dolly's untimely departure so many years before. In those seconds after, Jack subconsciously rekindled his thoughts, his dreams, and his imagination about what the crossing could possibly be like.

Yet even if he was ready today, he would have to wait. He wasn't quite prepared, but his body sure felt like it was. For the last few years, he had endured the pain, the hacking cough, and the brutal and surreal loneliness only losing the love of your life can bring. This time, this morning was not on his side. No, he would have to wait and put up with the aches, the pains, and the cruel and uncommon loneliness for just a few hours more.

Illusions and dreams had become quite frequent for him in his last few days. Whether he imagined his and Dolly's life when they were younger or the relentless rituals he created following her passing, lying in his bed provided the perfect and only respite for his imagination.

So like clockwork, his eyes opened to stare at the fan above. It could be morning or night, but in truth, it didn't matter. As his mind drifted once more, he rose from his bed and swung his feet around to ideally land on the carpet below. He stretched his arms upward and attempted to feel the carpet between his toes. He slowly and gingerly stood, in an attempt to gain his balance. With his balance secure, Jack made his way to his home office to continue his morning ritual.

Over the years since the day Dolly passed, Jack's quest to find spiritual signs delivered directly from her was all he sought and lived for. Whether it was butterflies fluttering through the wind, the sway of a tree branch, or the trusted cardinal swooping in on the unexpected morning, it didn't matter which one showed up. It was more of a hopeful expectation they would be the promised signs that everything would be okay.

Everyone told him the signs were real, but ironically, none of them ever seemed to show up on time when he searched. Day after day, he moped around attempting to convince himself he had seen one or all of them. In reality, his cynical mindset knew he had created an illusion. The signs were meant directly for him.

All the while, he knew deep down he had only fooled himself into believing his fictional account of his own illusions. The truth was that the signs he had picked were too coincidental. They were around anyway. And if they did show up, how could he really be sure it was her and not nature just being nature?

No, Jack always needed more proof. He needed that undeniable feeling that the signs were real and that she was still within reach of that familiar and comforting embrace. No matter how hard he pushed, he knew he needed more. As he rested his feet upon his office desk, he coughed and hacked as he stared out his window and waited.

The waiting always seemed like an eternity. The fact was, he really didn't know what he was waiting for, but nonetheless, he stared out the window for something. Periodically, a bird would fly by, or the wind would kick up, and Jack would try to convince himself they all had spiritual meaning.

He followed this routine for years, until finally he had enough. He needed to change his scenery. For him, it was all about what he would describe as "the art of distraction." Whether it was mindless television, endless surfing of the internet, or setting up travel to change his scenery, the idea to distract his mind from his actual reality of losing Dolly too soon became the only form of therapy he could muster. The continual interrupting of his thoughts by "going through the motions" of these events and activities became his only motivation of the day.

On the morning that everything would change, Jack gazed out his window to look once more for his next sign, but today, the sun was absent. The deafening silence within his ongoing and unfathomable void erupted, so he quickly turned on some music to start his day. Classic rock ruled the moment as his art of distraction took center stage. Kansas's timeless song "Carry On Wayward Son" emerged from his speaker. Jack lost himself in the familiar song as he closed his eyes and slipped away.

He was brought back to her bedside years before as he mindlessly stared. It was the same routine he had mastered for months, which had become a numbing exercise of surrealism. Helpless and completely drained, all he could do was glance over at the mere shell of the love of his life, who was moments from knocking on heaven's door. With every intention to remain alert, Jack fought hard to steal the glances, while uttering phrases of encouragement, until his eyes grew heavy.

For the first time in over eleven days, his fatigue won over. The battle she had endured baffled even the most seasoned nurses and clinicians. It was over eleven days in hospice. Ten of them lacked food, while seven of them lacked any form of fluids. The reality was that she was not willing to go just yet. Her pure will and love of her family kept her hanging on, regardless of the science behind it. Jack glanced once more as her mouth hung open and her heartbeat increased.

He tried desperately to keep his eyes open, but the lack of sleep finally overtook him as he gave in to his exhaustion and drifted into a much-needed slumber. Moments later, while startled by an odd clanking sound outside their room, Jack awoke and immediately looked over to his beloved. With the lights dimmed, he struggled to see clearly what had changed.

He slowly rose and anxiously stepped to her bedside. Her breathing had ceased, and her increased heartbeat was nonexistent. He quickly kissed her cheek, still warm. As he pulled himself away to gaze at his eternal soulmate, something odd came over him. He stared at her deeply and could not believe his eyes. Her gaunt appearance and open-mouthed struggle had been wonderfully transformed. Instead, Jack found himself staring at his beautiful wife, who had now gently closed her mouth and appeared to have a smile of contentment upon it.

Stunned at what he had experienced, he stepped away to clear his head and observe once more. Sure enough, she had a gentle smile of relief upon her face. It startled him even more that she had a unique and gentle glow. Her face shone with a golden hue of comforted softness he could not comprehend. As he stared in awe, the only logical explanation he could muster was that her years of suffering were now over. She was comfortably and happily resting in the arms of Jesus.

Still grief-stricken, Jack sat down next to the love of his life as the nurses and clinicians came in to record the time of passing. As the chaotic environment around them gained energy, he stared in amazement as he heard the classic Kansas tune of "Carry On Wayward Son," and he was brought back to his home office.

He gazed out his window and went back to search for his signs. Ultimately, he pulled out a faded photographic image from his wallet. It was Dolly, standing near a luau, holding two mai tais, waiting for someone. Jack stared at the image for what seemed like an eternity and simply smiled as he lost himself in one of his last morning moments.

Seconds later, he opened his eyes while lying in his bedroom staring at the fan above.

Chapter Two

The Luau

The strum of ukulele chords filtered through the lagoon as the mele chant from Hawaiian fire performers set the tone for the luau. This was their first time to Hawaii, and the islands did not disappoint. They were thoroughly enjoying what they called their second honeymoon. It's something about the Hawaiian Islands that miraculously transports you on a spiritual journey only moments after you visit. They had been on Maui for a few days by now, so their spirits were riding as high as they could get at this point.

She waited patiently for him, and as he walked from the restroom and into the luau's entrance, his eyes were transfixed on one thing and one thing only. There she was, standing with that welcoming spirit from the islands, looking as angelic and beautiful as ever. She wore a cute mango colored top with white knee-high pants as she held two mai tais in her hands. He stopped in awe and stared at her for a moment. It took his breath away as he marveled at her beauty and the gentle glow she reflected from the moonlight. He looked up at the moon and surveyed the surrounding lagoon. He finally gazed back at his lovely bride of over twenty-five years. He said to himself in a silent prayer-like manner, *Thank you, God, for this moment.*

Overtaken by the moment, he pulled his phone from his pocket and snapped a quick picture of her waiting for him, holding the drinks. As he put his phone away, he stared at her once more. The unforgettable moment seemed to last forever as the image of her waiting became etched upon his mind.

The lagoon faded away, but the image remained imprinted within his consciousness. Instead of at the lagoon walking toward his beautiful wife, Jack found himself back in his home office staring at the picture of her holding the drinks. The picture was now permanently the feature photo in his wallet as he sat somberly and stared at it.

The reality of this moment was that the picture had turned out to be his treasured captured memory of not only a beautiful trip but an incredible life shared with his one and only true soulmate. Problem was, this was all Jack had left. The memories, the pictures, and the videos had become his existence in the years following her passing.

He had never been truly motivated to accept the very real fact she was gone. The trip to Hawaii, the unbelievable, cherished life they shared, and their amazing family of Jack Jr., Annie, and Danny all seemed like a precious gift that was instantly stolen from them. Processing all of this was something he simply never could fathom. It became a ritual for him every morning as the chimes outside his window echoed their whimsical melodies of reminders.

Jack would sit at his desk, pray his rosary, listen to the chimes, and then religiously pull out the image of her standing holding the mai tais. It became a grueling but cherished routine which would start his day and end it for years. Still, it became the catalyst that fueled his unique search for the ultimate sign back to her.

Today, though, would be his last search for the signs. His mind fabricated a schedule full of doctors' appointments and prescription pickups as Annie, his daughter, was to be his chauffeur for the morning. As he stared out his window waiting for her car to pull up, a blue butterfly flew into view as Jack cynically smirked and said to himself, "Well, will you look at who's here." The butterfly fluttered for a few seconds and then flew off as Jack dismissed the encounter and opened his eyes to see the fan above his bed once more.

Chapter Three

The Sign

The fan blade rotated above with the familiar hum as Jack's hallucinations reminded him it was a monumental effort for him to move from room to room now. His aches, pains, and cough all contributed to the full-on effort for him to travel down the hall.

As he waited for Annie's car to pull up, his lack of patience and energy took over as he stood up and gingerly made the trek back toward his bedroom to lie down for a few moments while he waited.

In his ever-changing mind, Jack quickly determined his doctors' visits would have to wait today. Fact was, he had a pretty strong disdain for the healthcare community anyway, ever since Dolly's passing. In his mind, they never had a clue how to help her, but they sure did know how to charge her.

He figured, *Let them wait today.* In his opinion, the internet appeared to be a much more promising distraction than a physician's three-minute assessment of his current condition. He knew his body ached more every day for reasons he couldn't fathom, and what was a doctor really going to tell him at this stage anyway?

The internet seemed more appealing as he crept back into his bed and fired up his tablet. He instantly pulled up his Instagram account until only images of tropical settings appeared. He had seemed to stop and search these tropical images periodically, and the artificial intelligence (AI) algorithms from the internet mirrored his behavior. Tropical image after image were now served to his feed. It didn't take him long to get lost in each search.

Every now and then he would feed the AI algorithms extra hints of his hidden desires as he searched select keywords. Whether he typed in "signs from heaven" or "maps to your soulmate," the AI machines would pick up on his desires and feed him select images and videos of what he sought.

The pictures online increased with paradise, maps, and select signs until he keyed in on one unique image that piqued his interest. This one was far different and appeared to be tailored directly to him. The image was of an island bar set on a small peninsula. Within the picture, a small note featured his initials and a message. The message said, *"Join me at the Dock today and get ready to Soar."* The note pointed to the bar on the image and was signed, *"Love, God."*

Jack's heart skipped a beat as he stared at the image. *"Soar? Is this it? Is this the message I have sought for so many years?"* His heart raced uncontrollably. In his cynical state he told himself it was just another clever internet AI advertising move to sell something—but then again, this bar image looked familiar to him.

He stared at the bar until at last it hit him. He leaned over to his wallet which sat on his dresser and opened it to the image of his wife holding the mai tais. As he looked closely, he was floored to see that the bar behind her resembled the one in his new image. His heart skipped again as he leaned back against his headboard, rested his head upward, smiled, and said to himself, *It's time to Soar!*

Out of the corner of his eye, he saw his two sons, Jack Jr. and Danny, and his daughter, Annie, standing in the doorway. They looked at one another with concern as Jack Jr. said, "We have to try and get him up. He's gonna get bedsores."

Danny retort, "Just let him rest."

"No, I think we gotta try," Jack Jr. said.

They stared at their father in the bed, who seemed to completely ignore them. Annie gazed at him for a few seconds and said, "Maybe we should just let him be right now."

Jack glanced over, confused to see not only his three children but his entire family, with all his grandchildren and siblings, in the doorway as well. He asked, "Why is everyone over. Is there a party or something?"

None of the kids responded as they stared at him with frustration. Danny turned away and somberly said, "Let's just try later."

"I hate this!" Annie said as they each left the doorway.

As they left, Jack, again alone in his bed, finally glanced over and smiled with an odd smirk as he turned his phone toward the doorway, showing the image of the tropical bar with the note, and said, "It's time to *Soar!*"

Chapter Four

Liftoff

For the first time in what seemed like years, Jack felt stirred by a sense of relief. His cough had diminished a bit as the image of the bar and the note piqued something within him that he just had to follow. It was as if he was being drawn through his dark tunnel of despair toward a newfound destination of uncharted light pulling him onward.

He searched all the travel sites for the best last-minute offers until he found a special getaway deal on a charter flight called Sun Vacations that he could not pass up. The only caveat was that he had to leave quickly. With an odd sense of acceptance, he told himself it was okay to go ahead and booked the travel to his anticipated paradise without batting an eye.

He knew his kids might be sad he had left so abruptly, but it truly was out of his control at this stage. He was completely allured by this, and his motivation to learn more about the bar in paradise was the only thing on his mind.

Sooner than he thought, he found himself at the airport being flagged down by a guy with a sign featuring his name. Jack looked up and saw the MANDISA sign held high among the throng of escorts waiting by the gate. He walked toward the man holding the sign, and before he had an opportunity to notify him, the escort recognized him and said, "Welcome, Jack. We can't tell you how pleased we are you have arrived for your flight."

Surprised the escort knew him already, Jack responded, "Oh, ah—thank you."

The escort reached for Jack's carry-on bag and said, "I can take that for you."

Apprehensive, Jack leaned away and said, "Yeah, I read that in your travel itinerary about personal items. This is just some minor stuff I was taking with me on the flight. I'd like to keep it with me."

The escort smiled and said, "You don't need to bring anything with you on this flight. That's all taken care of." He continued to reach toward Jack's bag.

"Yeah, but—" Jack said, still resisting.

The escort cut him off and said, "It's okay. I'm telling you: you can't take it with you. Everything you need will be provided onboard."

Still reluctant, Jack looked around and noticed a few other passengers receiving similar treatment. All were reluctant but ultimately gave in to the unique instructions from the escorts.

"Okay, fine. Will you store it underneath?" Jack said agreeably.

"It will be stored," the escort said as he took Jack's bag and pointed him to the next section of the boarding process and said, "Follow this group here to your gate."

Confused and still a bit reluctant, Jack gave up the bag and slowly walked toward the group forming their line to board. As he walked toward the line, he could not help but notice the mix of people forming the line. They looked to be from all walks of life, with a visible diversity among the group. He took his place at the end as more people quickly came to follow him. Jack waited patiently as the line stood still for a while. He gazed up and down the line as most kept to themselves, waiting for the onboarding process to begin.

Finally, after a few moments of curious voyeurism within the crowd, the traveler behind Jack said, "Why are you here?"

Startled, Jack turned back to the man and said, "Excuse me?" The man stood at six feet five and towered over him.

"Sorry, I'm Michael. This line, this trip. I'm guessing you really needed this to pay what you did for it," the man said.

"I'm Jack," he replied. Confused, he went on, "How would you know what I paid?"

"Believe me, everyone in this line paid an arm and a leg for this ticket. Just curious what brought you here."

The line started to move as the boarding process commenced. Reluctant to go into detail, Jack said, "Well, that's a long story. Let's just say I really needed it."

"Don't we all, my friend. Well, looks like we're moving. Enjoy your trip," the man said as they each took tiny steps to move forward.

"Thanks; you too," Jack said as he followed the line toward the boarding gate.

Jack watched as the gatekeeper scanned their tickets and passengers walked through the gates. As he made it to the agent, he pulled his phone out of his pocket and tapped it to display his ticket. As he scanned it, a blue light illuminated within the scanner as the gate agent said, "Welcome aboard Sun Vacations. Enjoy your trip, Mr. Mandisa."

Jack glanced up at the enthusiastic agent and said, "Ah—thank you." He continued onto the gate ramp and walked toward the flight's entrance. He felt something odd within him as he instinctively raised his right hand and gestured to perform the sign of the cross. As soon as he completed the gesture, he found himself at the entrance of the plane with the flight attendants eagerly waiting for their next set of passengers.

"Welcome," the first attendant said as Jack stepped onto the plane.

"Thank you," he said. He walked through the entranceway and turned to view his gate ticket one last time to verify his seat. He confirmed his seat was row 37, seat A.

He looked back up to view the plane and continued to walk the aisle. As he strolled down the aisle, he grew more puzzled, as all the seats in the plane appeared to be first class.

He kept on walking and waiting for the coach seats to appear, which never happened. "They're all first class?" he murmured to himself.

"I told you, an arm and a leg," Michael said as he scooted past Jack and sat down in seat 37-B.

"I guess so," Jack said, stopping in front of row 37.

"Hey, looks like we're neighbors," Michael said. "Good thing we got plenty of room, right? I'm kind of a big guy, you know."

"Yeah, that you are," Jack said as he slowly settled into his seat next to Michael.

As customary in first class, the flight attendants were in high customer service mode, but this time for the entire plane. From the drinks and snacks offered before takeoff to the hot towels, Jack was quickly warming up to this unique and special treatment.

"This is unbelievable," he said. "I don't think I've ever seen first class like this. They're serving everyone."

Michael looked over with a handful of snacks shoved into his mouth and repeated, "An arm and a leg, man."

Jack chuckled and said, "Yeah," shaking his head

They both settled in, and before he knew it, the flight had taken off. Michael looked over to him and said, "Here we go."

Chapter Five

In the Process

The flight's scheduled airtime was approximately five hours. With two and a half hours already shaved off, Jack had settled into his first-class flight with flying colors. He enjoyed the wining and dining immensely as the drinks and fresh prepared food kept coming.

As he continued to enjoy his surf and turf, he looked over at Michael, who had fallen asleep. As he glanced around the rest of the plane, the other passengers appeared to be enjoying their own customized meal experiences, and for the first time in a long time, Jack felt a sense of calm. He took a deep breath as he sipped his glass of wine and took in the peaceful moment while enjoying his meal and said to himself, *Man, I needed this.*

He continued to nibble his food as he tinkered with the video monitor in front of him. He went through each channel offering on the tablet displayed. He scrolled through the movie channels, the sports channel, and even took some time watching the route of the plane on the GPS navigator. After about twenty minutes of mindlessly surfing, he noticed the option of Bluetooth connection. "Huh?" he grunted as he clicked on the feature and realized he was able to sync his phone up and into the monitor.

He glanced back over to Michael, who was still sleeping.

As the monitor connected with his phone, Jack did what he had always done when he had time on his hands. He went back to his own photo and video app, which ultimately featured his family, his life, and—most important to him—his beautiful wife, Dolly. He started to scroll through the images first and keyed in on some recent pictures of him and his kids. He smiled as he reminisced on the photos of his kids and all his young grandchildren. He filtered through the years until he pulled up an image of his wife, Dolly. He immediately stopped scrolling and just stared at the image in his melancholy manner. As he stared at her, he lost himself for a moment until he heard a voice saying, "She's pretty."

Startled, Jack turned and noticed Michael looking at the image. "What?"

"She's pretty. Who is she?" Michael said.

A bit apprehensive, Jack said, "Ah—that's, uh—that was my wife."

Michael stared at the image and said, "Was?"

"Yeah, she passed," Jack said.

Michael said, "Huh? I'd still say is. I never really believed in 'was.'"

Jack stared at Michael and thought for a second. Then he said, "Yeah … I kinda like that. Is, it is." He smiled and quickly turned off his Bluetooth to take the images off the monitor.

"Oh, I didn't mean to disrupt you. Please continue," Michael said.

"No, I'm good. No worries," Jack said

"I'm serious. I didn't mean to eavesdrop," Michael said.

"I was kinda done anyway," Jack said. "Actually, I think I spend too much time staring at those images anyway. Not sure it's for the best."

"What do you mean?" Michael replied.

"I don't know," Jack said. "Ever since she passed, it's all I seem to do. It helps me at times, but most of the time it makes me miss her more."

"Yes, I can see that. Well, take a break then. You can always go back."

"Yeah—yeah, I do, and I will," Jack replied as he clicked the monitor to project the GPS image of the flight once more.

"About halfway there, huh?" Michael said.

"Looks like it."

"What's bringing you to the islands?" Michael said.

Jack paused for a moment and with a slight smirk on his face, he showed him the image of his wife.

Confused, Michael said, "I don't understand."

"It's a bit crazy, but we vacationed there a long time ago, and for some reason I feel I'm being drawn back. Kinda like she's there, waiting for me. I know it's nuts, but there's been these signs, and I don't know. It is crazy. Maybe I just needed a vacation. This place just reminds me of her and the great time we had together."

"Huh," Michael said.

"It does sound crazy, doesn't it?"

"Well, not totally."

Jack smiled and said, "You're too kind."

"No, I'm serious. I kinda get it. Well, I will tell you this, you picked the right carrier to get you there. Can't go wrong with Sun Vacations."

"I know, but costs you that arm and leg huh?" Jack said, laughing.

Michael laughed and replied, "Sure does."

The two men resumed their individual time killing-habits as they both went back to their reading. Jack stayed on his phone as Michael pulled out a book. The book was titled, *When You Get There.*

Soon the flight attendants came through once more with their mid-flight snacks. Still amazed about the customer service, Jack accepted the snacks wholeheartedly and settled into the next leg of the trip.

Distracted by just about everything, he couldn't settle. He tinkered with his phone for a few more moments and then went back to the monitors in front of him. Finally, after a few moments he glanced over to Michael's book and said, "What's that about?"

Michael looked at him and said, "It's sort of a guide. You'll get one too."

"Me? Why me?"

"Can't expect to know everything when you arrive," Michael explained. "This will help some."

"Can I take a look?" Jack asked.

"Not just yet," Michael said as he resumed his reading.

Confused, Jack said, "What's that supposed to mean?"

"Means what it means. You're not ready, Jack."

"Not ready? Not ready for what?"

"That reunion you're seeking." Michael said.

"What are you talking about?"

"Might be good for you to go back to some of your videos once more. It's always good to reminisce. It's good for the soul."

"I'm really confused here," Jack said. "Who are you? Do I know you?"

"You might say we've known each other forever," Michael said.

"What? I don't understand."

Michael closed his book and stared directly into Jack's eyes. "Jack, you're in the process of dying."

Jack looked at Michael and slowly laughed. "I'm in the process of what? That's great. Dying, huh?"

Michael didn't say a word. He let Jack soak in his statement a bit more.

Jack looked around the plane and cynically laughed as he shook his head in disbelief and said to himself, *I guess that's what I get for sharing too much with strangers.*

Michael still didn't react to Jack. He continued to stare at him with a reassuring grin.

Jack looked around once more and then looked at Michael. He felt increasingly uncomfortable as Michael sat motionless. Finally, Jack said, "Who are you?"

"I told you, my name is Michael and you can say, I'm somewhat of a guardian for you."

"A guardian? For me?"

"Yeah. I know this is a lot to process, but the transition can sometimes be tricky."

"You're serious, aren't you?

"Do you remember getting to the airport? Michael asked.

Jack thought for a moment and said, "Ah—yeah. My kids took me. No—wait a second …." He kept on thinking.

"You kind of just showed up, didn't you?" Michael said.

Jack thought it over again. He tried to remember how he'd arrived at the airport and could not come up with it. In fact, the last thing he could remember was lying in his bed searching for vacation deals as his kids ignored and spoke over him.

As he gathered himself, he looked back up to Michael and said, "Where am I?"

Michael gazed back at him and replied, "You're on your way, Jack, but not before your review."

"My what?"

"You were given a very special gift of existence a short time ago. It's time to take-a-look and see how you treated that very special gift."

Unsure how to take it all in, Jack said, "I—um, I—I'm not sure I understand."

"You will. You're about to go on the journey of a lifetime, your lifetime!"

"My lifetime?" Jack said.

"We'll be landing soon. Also, a few of my friends will be joining us once we land to help you on the way. What do you say we get a little rest now?"

"What?" Jack said, confused, as Michael placed his book on his lap and closed his eyes.

With his head spinning, all Jack could do was scan the plane and the passengers as his mind went into a million directions trying to absorb the surreal discussion he had just gone through.

Chapter Six

The Flight

Michael was asleep next to Jack as the flight attendant's voice filled the plane. "Please prepare for landing." Jack looked around and wasn't sure what to make of this environment.

Everything around him felt real. The food tasted amazing, the drinks were so refreshing, and the people in each seat appeared as normal as possible. They sure didn't look like ghosts to him. This Michael character next to him had to be playing games.

Sure, he didn't remember getting to the airport, but that could be explained, especially the way he had been feeling the last few weeks. Jack looked around as the flight attendants prepared for landing and glanced back at Michael, who was out like a light.

As he looked over, Michael still had the *When You Get There* book on his lap. Curious, Jack leaned over to gain a better view of the cover. As he leaned over, the airplane shook with slight turbulence.

Jack leaned back as the flight leveled off and watched as the attendants made their final run through the cabin, cleaning up before landing. Still asleep, Michael moved slightly to gain a more comfortable position, and the book slid off his lap and onto the floor in front of them. Jack immediately noticed and looked around as if he had done something mischievous. Instinctively, he reached down and grabbed hold of the book as the plane's turbulence increased once more.

As he shook with the plane, Jack pulled the book up from the floor and glanced over to Michael. He was still asleep as the turbulence increased. Nervous, as if he were a young child trying to get away with stealing a pack of gum, Jack checked Michael again as he tried to open the cover of the book. As he took hold of the binding, the plane shook more aggressively, and the passengers aboard started to get uneasy. Concerned as well, Jack immediately looked up and noticed a dark, ominous mist floating within the cabin near him. The mist hovered close to him as the turbulence continued.

Unsure what to do, Jack felt dizzy as his hand grabbed the binding even tighter to pull open the cover. The plane shook uncontrollably, and chaos within the cabin peaked. Suddenly Jack, nearly unconscious now, felt Michael's oversized hand slam down the cover and close the book.

Jack immediately blacked out.

"Dad, it's okay to rest now. We are all here." Jack heard the voice of Annie, his daughter, as he tried feverishly to open his eyes.

"Hey, Dad, it's Jack Jr. Look who's here with me. It's little Jackie. He wanted to spend some time with his Papa."

Responding within his own consciousness, Jack fought to open his mouth but his eyes felt glued shut as he answered each and every one of them who screamed out his name, but no words physically came out of his mouth.

For what seemed like the next few hours, Jack felt the pains, the aches, and the discomfort he had grown so accustomed to over the years as he heard his family talking directly to him as well as to each other within his bedroom.

The conversations went in many directions. Some were directed to him, and some were random, dealing with mini family events and minor crises that often arose. Jack laughed internally as he listened to their sometimes-trivial trials and ordeals they all appeared to be overwhelmed with. As he listened, what seemed to be important and concerning yesterday really didn't seem to mean the same today. Jack had an odd comfort at listening to their problems, feeling they were not really problems at all. He knew internally that the challenges his family discussed around him were trivial.

As time went on, people came in and out of the room. Jack could sense them all but never could open his shut eyes or speak directly to them. It was as if he was in the room but also floating above to witness it all. Then, suddenly, he heard his familiar classic rock music within his room which calmed his body as a sudden flush of adrenaline shot through his spirit.

Within seconds his body shook, and he once more felt the turbulence of the plane as he heard, "Prepare for landing."

Startled by it all, Jack looked around and saw the familiar passengers in the plane. He glanced over to his right and saw Michael staring at him. "I told you, you're just not ready yet. You can get this after your review," Michael said, as he held up the *When You Get There* book.

Jack, still a bit stunned by everything, looked at Michael and asked, "Where am I?"

"I told you. You're transitioning," Michael said. "Takes a little to get comfortable, but just trust the process. All will be good."

Jack stared at him and said, "Am I dying?"

"Prepare for landing," the flight attendant said over the intercom.

"It is what they customarily call it, but it's not really what I would call it," Michael replied as he smiled and placed the book in his backpack.

Jack looked around the plane and said to himself, *What is going on?*

Michael looked back at him as the plane touched down on the tarmac and said, "A couple of my colleagues will be taking you from here. We'll touch base later. Remember, trust in the process."

Still uneasy and confused, Jack said, "What is the process?"

"Just trust in it. I'll see you later." Michael got up, gathered his backpack, and got in line to deboard the plane.

Jack sat in his seat, still unsure what to do next. As the passengers deboarded, he slowly stood and gingerly started to follow.

Chapter Seven

Across the Jetway

As he passed through the plane's door, Jack felt alone for a split second. The jetway was dimly lit and looked like a long runway of darkness. He was the last to deplane. Motivated only by his curiosity, he followed the line in front of him.

Step by step, Jack followed for about twelve feet. Suddenly, a sliver of light shone from the terminal ahead. Once he saw the light at the end of the jetway, his mood changed. With every step he took toward the exit, a flush of adrenaline flowed through him.

Oddly, with every footstep, he felt more youthful. The aches and the pains he had grown so accustomed to were vanishing as he approached the terminal. Stunned by the overwhelming feeling of youthful vitality, he stretched and moved his joints in ways he hadn't done in years. The simple clenching and spreading of his hands provided more joy than he could fathom at this point. He couldn't remember the last time he had flexed his hands without incredible numbness and pain. As he kept walking, not only could he open and close his hands without pain, but his entire body had a flush of healed rejuvenation he could not have imagined.

As the jetway shortened, the illumination near the exit also increased. It became obvious to Jack as he neared the exit that the end of the ramp was outside, and the illumination he was walking toward was the sun.

Uniquely, the bright light from outside was striking but not harsh upon his eyes as he made it to the step down from the jetway. Even though the sun shone directly upon him, he did not feel the need to squint at all. Jack marveled at the feeling upon his eyes as well as his invigorated joints and had to stop for a moment to take in the surreal environment spread before him.

This is unbelievable, he said to himself as he took a step forward and into the opened air terminal in front of him. As he walked into the terminal, he could immediately smell the fresh fragrances of sweet fruits and vegetation nearby. Palm trees and fresh-cut green grass awaited him only a few feet away. He immediately noticed the passengers were all taking their shoes off to experience the lush carpet of grass beneath their toes. Curious, he looked around and instinctively decided to kick off his shoes and socks as well. He walked up to the grass and placed his foot upon it. A rush of a cool mint tingle shot though his body and provided a sense of relief unlike anything he had ever felt. He placed his other foot down and felt it once more. The sensations made his former aches and pains unimaginable at this point. He continued to walk upon the grass without a care of leaving his shoes behind. As he took a deep breath, he stopped to gaze at the amazing outdoor terminal in front of him. He did not feel cold or warm. The temperature felt perfect. The crystal air was clear, pure, and sweet smelling. The beauty of it all was astonishing to him.

As he looked around, he saw the varied passengers speaking to new sets of guides waiting for them on the grass. He watched as they spoke for a few moments and then walked away together toward the minibuses nearby.

"Hi, Jackie?" Jack heard from behind him. He turned around and saw a woman in her early thirties standing behind him. It took him a second to process, but he knew her.

"Aunt Carol?" he said hesitantly.

"Welcome, Jack, we're so glad you're here," she said.

"Is that really you? You look fabulous," Jack said.

"Thank you, Jackie," she said. "The environment here does seem to bring the best out of us."

"But you died so many years ago. I remember it so vividly."

"As do I," Aunt Carol said, "but I'm here right now to help you through your assessment phase. They felt a familiar face right now can help to ease some of your intro."

"Assessment phase?" Jack asked. "What does that mean? Is Dolly here? Please tell me she's here."

"It's not that she's not here, Jackie; it's that you are not quite all here yet. You're still in transition, honey. That's where the assessment comes in."

"What is that supposed to mean? I'm here. I feel like I'm here. And I don't need any assessment. Please, Aunt Carol, just let me see Dolly."

Aunt Carol smiled with a reassuring grin and grabbed his hand. "Just trust in the process, Jackie."

Jack looked around as she held his hand and saw the other passengers leaving on buses. "Where are they going? Can one of those take me to see her?"

"You're going to take one. Just a little more patience," she replied.

He looked at her with sympathetic eyes and said, "Aunt Carol, I really do not need any assessment. Please just point me in her direction."

She looked at him and smiled with a reassuring gaze and said, "Here comes your bus." She also noticed behind him the same dark mist cloud which was on the plane. The cloud hovered behind Jack. As Aunt Carol saw the mist she frowned slightly.

Jack turned and saw a bus drive up toward him. He turned back toward her and said, "Okay, but—" She had vanished. The dark mist cloud was also gone.

"Aunt Carol? Aunt Carol?" he said as he looked around the area as the bus came to a stop in front of him. The door opened as the bus driver said, "Ready to go?"

Confused, he surveyed the terminal and in an agreeable mode said, "Yeah, yeah, I'm ready." He stepped onto the bus and sat down. The doors to the bus closed, and they drove off.

Chapter Eight

Check-In

Jack found himself staring out of a French door balcony off a presidential suite, which overlooked a picturesque resort property. Much like arriving at the airport, he couldn't recall his ride from the tarmac to the resort. One moment he boarded the bus, and moments later he found himself in a robe enjoying the first-class room service in his lavish new suite.

As he stared out the window and into the breathtaking view in front of him, he reached over to a bowl of fresh strawberries on his table on the balcony. He picked up an oversized berry and dipped it in a nearby bowl of yogurt and bit into the luscious treat. As he savored the amazing flavors from the fruit and yogurt combination, he looked around his surreal environment and was overwhelmed by its beauty. *This is unbelievable*, he said to himself as he continued to enjoy the various treats and room service delicacies left in his room.

His room was set on the highest perch of the resort. The height of the room allowed for him to see the breadth of the property which seemed to go on forever. It was simply awe-inspiring. As far as he could see, the beauty and the tranquility of the peninsula was made for a paradise unlike anything he could ever imagine.

As the tropical birds flew and a gentle wind flowed across the land, Jack stared into the crystal blue waters below. He saw dolphins frolic and manta rays soar through the waters. The waters were so clear that he could see the bottom hundreds of yards out. Just outside his room was the most amazing holm oak tree shaped into a perfectly rounded umbrella. The tree was massive and just beyond was the serene sea waters below.

"I cannot believe how gorgeous this is!" he said to himself as he stood marveling on the balcony. He stayed outside for an extended period of time, but it didn't seem to register with him how long he was out there. The tranquility of the environment infused a sense of calm within him, and he could have stared at it forever.

As he watched the dolphins leap into a rainbow mist, he was distracted by an open deck boat careening across the waters toward a small land mass off the coast. As he moved on the balcony to gain a better look, the dark mist that had appeared on the plane and along with his Aunt Carol was now hovering in his room behind him. Unaware of the mist behind him, Jack moved to the edge of the balcony to look. He also reached down for another strawberry, but this time as he grabbed hold of the fruit, he felt an ache in his hand. This ache was familiar to him; he had grown so accustomed to these pains for so many years.

Surprised it had come back, he looked at his hand and shook it to gain his feeling back. Within seconds, his other hand felt the same ache. "What is going on here?" he said as he tried to shake the pain away. As he shook and rubbed his extremities to gain the feeling, the dark mist within his room had crept closer to him. Still unaware of the intruding mist, Jack frustratingly tried to ignore his renewed pains as he strained to gain a better glimpse of the distraction in the sea.

As he looked and peered in the distance at the boat traveling across the tranquil waters, the dark mist behind him came closer. With each inch nearer, Jack felt more pain. Seconds later, his cough returned as he hacked and bent over to find relief. The intensity of the cough increased as he finally turned to the inside of his room and saw the dark mist, which was now hovering above him. "What in the—?" he said.

Seconds later, Jack's cough was now uncontrollable as his eyes opened and he found himself staring at his familiar ceiling fan back in his bedroom. His family hovered over him as he heard his son Danny say, "His eyes, they just opened."

"Oh my God—hi, Dad," Annie said as she rushed up close to his bedside.

Unsure what was happening, Jack internally felt pleased to see his kids and family but also felt an extreme anxiety at being separated from where he had just left. He groaned and shook his head in frustration as his kids maneuvered to get closer.

"It's okay, Dad. We're all here. Everyone is by your side," Annie said as the family came closer and tried to communicate with him.

Jack could make out what they were saying but at the same time kept shaking his head as he lifted his arm and abruptly said, "Dolly, where's Dolly? Just show me her."

Taken aback by his outburst, Jack Jr. said, "He's talking about Mom again."

"You think he sees her?" Annie asked.

"Who's knows what they see at this stage?" Danny said. "But he's reaching for something, that's for sure."

"I believe that. I believe that he sees her. It's okay, Dad," Annie encouraged him. "Keep reaching for Mom. She is close to you now." She grabbed hold of his other hand to comfort him.

Jack let out another outburst, screaming, "Dolly!"

"I think we need to say a prayer over him. It may calm him down," Danny said.

"Okay, good idea. What should we say?" Annie asked.

Danny thought for a moment and said, "How 'bout the 'Our Father'?"

"Perfect. You lead," she said.

"Okay, sure." Danny looked around the room with all their loved ones hovered over Jack and said, "Everyone come closer."

They all responded and came close to Jack and created a circle around him. Some of them grabbed each other's hands as some of them rested their hands on their shoulders in comfort. All three of Jack's kids grabbed hold of his hand as they all joined in the prayer: "Our Father, who art in heaven, hallowed be thy name; thy kingdom come; thy will be done on earth as it is in heaven. Give us this day our daily bread; and forgive us our trespasses as we forgive those who trespass against us; and lead us not into temptation but deliver us from evil."

As they finished the prayer, they all stood around and watched as Jack calmed down from his outbursts and pain flare-ups and gently closed his eyes. His kids looked at one another with comfort as Annie said, "Let's let him rest."

"Okay. I'd like to stay, though," Jack Jr. said. "Why don't each of us take some time to be by ourselves with him for a bit? I can go first."

"Yeah, I like that," Annie replied as they dispersed to allow for each of the kids to share some time alone with Jack.

Jack's eyes were now fully shut again as he drifted once more.

Chapter Nine

The Atrium

Tropical birds flew past the balcony as Jack woke from his slumber and realized he was back in his presidential suite, lying on his oversized luxury bed. He sat up and gazed out his opened window off the balcony and could see the amazing holm oak tree with its massive, perfectly rounded umbrella shape.

He stood up and immediately noticed his aches and pains had ceased once more. He opened and closed his hands and nodded with pleasure. He strolled back over to the balcony and stood on its perch to take in the view again. As he marveled at the views, he saw the dolphins and manta rays below as well as another open deck boat careening across the waters heading over to the land mass off the peninsula.

He watched this activity for a while and counted a half dozen boats making the trip across the bay. Intrigued by everything, he tried to calm himself down as his mind wandered in many directions, unsure what was actually going on.

Suddenly, he heard the phone ring in his suite. He turned away from the views and went inside the suite to pick up the phone. "Hello," Jack said.

"You up for a drink?" the voice said.

"Excuse me? Who is this?" Jack asked.

"It's Michael, from the plane. You think you can pull yourself away from what you're doing for a cocktail?"

"Ah—yeah. Sure, I guess," Jack replied.

"Great, meet downstairs. I'm at the bar," Michael said as he hung up the phone.

"Okay—hello?" Jack said as he heard the click of the phone. He stared at the phone for a second and thought, *Why not, right?*

Jack hung up and looked around for his clothes. All he could find was a pair of white linen pants and a turquoise blue button-down beach shirt in his closet. "When in Rome," he said as he reached into the closet and pulled out the clothes.

After he was dressed, he looked around for a pair of shoes, but nothing could be found. Finally, after searching a bit, he gave up and decided to leave the room barefoot. He left his room and strolled down the hallway toward the elevators, and without his pushing any buttons, the elevator doors opened upon his arrival.

"Hmm, okay," Jack said as he stepped inside. He looked around as the doors closed and could not find any buttons. He felt the elevator move on its own without any prompting from him. Within seconds, the doors opened, and he found himself on the first-floor lobby. *That was pretty quick*, he said to himself as he tentatively walked out of the elevator.

As he stepped out, he made his way into a grand entrance of a miraculous lobby which was half indoors and outdoors. The tropical setting within the atrium was breathtaking. It was as if he was walking into a paradise setting unlike any high-end resort can reproduce.

Anywhere he looked, he was overtaken by the tranquility and beauty. He strolled through the entrance and marveled at the magnificence of

the setting. The flowers and the trees within the atrium cc
the various fountains and waterfalls sprinkled through th

As he followed the path, it took him to the center oɪ ᴛɦᴇ ᴀᴛɪᴜɪɪɪ
which featured a large oval-shaped bar. Sitting at the bar holding a
tropical drink was Michael. He waved to Jack as he took a sip of his
cocktail.

Jack acknowledged Michael and walked up to him. "What are you
drinking?" Michael asked as he pointed toward the bar.

Jack looked up and down the bar and said to the bartender nearby,
"Um—hi, how ya doing? You know, I think I'll have an old-fashioned.
It's been that kind of day."

"Old-fashioned coming up," the bartender said.

Michael moved slightly to allow for Jack to sit down next to him on
a barstool. "This is quite a resort," Jack said.

"It's something, huh?" Michael replied.

"Old-fashioned," the bartender said as he placed Jack's drink on
the bar.

"Wow, that was quick!" Jack said.

"Enjoy!" the bartender said as he wiped the counter near him and
moved away from the two men.

Jack looked at the drink and settled into his barstool. He took a deep
breath and sipped the drink. Then he looked over to Michael. "Can you
please tell me what's going on here?"

Michael looked up from his drink and scanned the bar. "I believe
it's happy hour."

Jack looked over cynically and said, "Come on. Where am I,
Michael? What is going on with me?"

"I told you on the plane. You're going through transition," Michael
replied.

"Transition? What's transition?" Jack asked.

"It's kind of like you're here, but you're not," Michael said. "Like a half-baked pie."

"A half-baked pie? That's what you're telling me? Is this Heaven? Am I dead?"

Michael started to laugh. "This? Is this Heaven? Oh no. Close, but not quite there yet."

"This is close? Man, this is a paradise," Jack said.

"You should see Heaven," Michael said.

Jack looked at Michael with concern and said, "Will I?"

"Just let the process work through. You will see," Michael assured him.

"I don't understand. What is the process? What do I have to do?" Jack asked.

"You really don't have to do anything," Michael replied. "I mean, most of it you have already done."

"I've done most of what? What do you mean?"

"It'll all come out. Don't you worry. How's your drink?"

"My drink? My drink is fine, but wait a second," Jack said, his concern rising. "How should I not worry? What have I done? Did I do something wrong? Am I in jeopardy?"

"*Jeopardy!*—oh, that really is a great show," Michael said. "As for you, no jeopardy, just a little talking."

"Talking about what?" Jack said.

"Well, we can start with you."

"Me?"

"Yeah, tell me something I should know about you," Michael said.

"I don't know. I mean, like what?"

"What motivates you? What keeps you going?"

"What motivates me? Ha!" Jack said sarcastically.

"Why do you laugh?"

"Because I haven't been motivated for years."

"Really? How could that be?" Michael asked.

"To be honest with you, I lost any ounce of motivation and desire, the day my Dolly left me," Jack replied.

"Is that right?"

"It's true. I don't know if you ever had someone who truly was your everything, and then one day that everything was ripped from you. It breaks you. I don't care how tough someone may think they are; believe me, it breaks you!"

"She sounds like she was pretty special," Michael said.

"You have no idea," Jack replied.

"How did you guys meet—and not for anything, who was the six-pack?

Surprised, Jack looked at him and said, "The six-pack? How do you know about the six-pack?"

Michael looked over with a slight smile and said, "Kinda my job to know some of these things."

"Yeah, I guess it is," Jack said.

"So tell me about them. Were they involved in how you guys met?" Michael asked.

"They sure were, but I suppose you already know that."

"Maybe, but I love a good love story. Go on."

Jack looked at Michael and smiled. He then motioned to the bartender and said, "I'll take another one of these."

"So who were the six-pack?" Michael asked.

Jack received another drink from the bartender and settled in to tell his story of the six-pack.

Chapter Ten

The Six-Pack and the Red Wristbands

"It's funny. Dolly and I probably would have never met if it weren't for the six-pack."

"How so?" Michael said.

"Well, my buddies and I were going to this thing called the Party in the Park," Jack said. "It was this festival-type thing downtown where some great local and national bands would play. I was just going out for another night with the guys when we were walking across the street and this car with six cute women almost hit us. One of my buddies knew one of the girls, so they stopped and spoke briefly."

"Was Dolly in the car?" Michael asked.

"Oh yeah, she was. In fact, even though all these girls were very cute, I honed-in on one thing and one thing only. She was in the back seat, and I could not take my eyes off her. Their car only stopped for a minute, but I was struck."

"It was a love-at-first-sight thing, huh?" Michael said.

"It sure was. It got even better later that day." Jack replied.

"How so?" Michael asked.

"We kind of did the bar crawl thing at the various spots playing music that day, but we ended up at the Rock House, which was a local university bar. We did the typical trolling young guys do in these types of bars. And to be honest with you, I really believe I was ready to find my soulmate that night. I remember it so vividly. I walked into the main bar area, and standing near the jukebox by a lounge area was Dolly. She was surrounded by her five other cute friends, but it was as if a cloud hovered around her, and she was the only thing I saw."

"Man, you were struck," Michael said.

"One hundred percent. It was so natural too. Our eyes met, and I went over to talk, and it was like we had known each other forever. Our conversation was so effortless and easy. We laughed and talked and laughed even more. It was like talking to my best friend I'd had for years. The night passed us by without a blink. Before we knew it, the bar was closing, and everyone was getting ready to go. This is where the six-pack came into play."

"What did they do? Michael asked.

"You must understand, these girls grew up together, through elementary, middle, and high school," Jack said. "They were closer to one another than even some of their family members. They had each other's back and sometimes would even finish each other's sentences. And believe me, this was evident in how they protected one another as the men would troll by during the evening. Well, everyone was getting ready to go, and I naturally asked Dolly for her phone number."

"Seems reasonable," Michael responded.

"You would think, but she was just coming off a breakup from high-school and was nervous. Not wanting to lose this opportunity, I worked it hard for a few more tries in front of the entire six-pack but couldn't get the number. As the night was ending, we were all saying our goodbyes, and one of her best friends, Lily, snuck up to me and handed me her number and said, 'Call her. I know she wants you to.' It was like a formal endorsement. If one of the six-pack approved, it was okay."

"She just gave you the number?" Michael said.

"Yes, it was perfect. I was on cloud nine. And you know what? I told my buddy that night that I was going to marry her. I just knew it. It was that immediate feeling, and that emotion has never left me. And the six-pack, who I think I named that night, became an important part of our lives in every way."

"How so?" Michael said.

"Well, like I told you, they were a tight bonded group of girls who literally were there for every moment of each other's lives. They truly had each other's back and were involved in pretty much everything. When Dolly and I started dating, we were inseparable. In most cases, some friends would get frustrated by something like that, but not this group. If they knew one of their six was happy, they all supported it. We all ended up in each other's weddings, became godparents to each other's kids and vacationed through the years as a group."

"Sounds like a special friendship."

"Nothing really like it," Jack said. "We were blessed to be able to have this group through the years. The amazing part of it was as each one of the girls found their soulmate, they seemed to fit the group perfectly. All the guys got along like brothers, and you can argue we could have changed the name from the six-pack to the twelve-pack through the years, but that wouldn't have been right. No, the girls deserved their own branding. They were unique, and their bond never faded."

"Pretty amazing. You don't often seem to hear someone talk that way about friends."

"Truth is, they all became more than friends. They became family, especially when Dolly got sick."

"That's great, really great," Michael said. "We'll get to that later though. I want to hear more about Dolly before she got sick."

Jack took a sip of his drink and stared out into the amazing views in front of him and said, "Okay, sure. Thing is, it's been hard to shake it over the years. It's as if that's all I ever could think about."

"Seems like you may have been focusing on the wrong things," Michael said.

Jack thought for a moment and said, "Yeah, you're probably right. But like I told you, it controls you when you're broken. I used to laugh when people used to tell me time heals. That is such a load of crap. Believe me, time has nothing to do with it. In fact, for me, it became more real every day. It made that next day even more unbearable and kept on confirming she was really gone."

"But was she really gone?" Michael asked.

"Well, she sure wasn't in the house anymore," Jack replied.

Michael sat back and looked at him perplexed. "Really?"

"Well, I mean not physically. I guess everywhere you looked, her presence was there, but she wasn't."

"Huh?" Michael said.

"You can't understand if you haven't experienced it," Jack said.

"Well maybe, understanding is experiencing it," Michael responded.

Jack tried to absorb Michael's wisdom but was still quite confused. He took another sip of his drink and said, "I guess so." He put his drink on the bar and looked around the property and at a few other people around the bar. They all seemed to be great moods.

It was as if they were all on vacation and had met around the bar for cocktail hour, just before starting their evening. They were all dressed to the nines as if they were going out for dinner, and each one of them was as cheerful as they could be.

"There's a lot of people here. And none of them have shoes," Jack said.

Michael looked at the group around the bar and said, "It's a pretty popular place, and shoes are a bit overbearing, don't you think?"

"I suppose," Jack said. "Where are they all going? It seems like they are all getting ready for something."

"Some of them are, and some of them may have to stay back," Michael said.

"But where are they going?" Jack asked.

Distracted, Michael looked away and said, "Excuse me, Jack, I'll be back in a bit." He got up from his bar chair and walked toward a woman holding a clipboard tablet near a sushi bar.

"Oh, okay, sure," Jack said as Michael got up and walked over to the woman. He watched as Michael listened intently to the woman, who was pointing to items on her tablet.

After a few seconds, Jack lost interest in the two and once more scanned the people around the bar. He marveled at the jovial nature of the people and their cocktail hour demeanor. It looked so enticing to him as his enthusiasm grew every second he observed.

"You going over too, buddy?" Jack heard a voice to his right and saw a man sitting on a barstool near him. The man looked to be in his late thirties and was sipping an espresso martini. The man was dressed in beach attire and an oversized straw hat; the string dangled around his neck. Jack said, "Excuse me?"

"The name's Nick. How you doing? Are you going over today?" Nick asked.

Realizing he was talking to him, Jack reached his hand out to shake it and said, "Going over where?"

"To the dock, I suppose," Nick said as if he should already know the location.

Jack looked at him, perplexed, and said, "The dock? So what exactly is the dock?"

Nick chuckled and said, "Apparently, the place everyone wants to be. I guess most everyone's going over."

Jack looked into the sea below them and said, "You know, I've been watching that outside my window in my room. Is that where that boat's been going?"

"Yeah, sure is," Nick said. "Guess you haven't read about it?"

"Read about it? No. Where would I read about it?" Jack asked.

"It's all in the welcoming packet," Nick replied.

Confused, Jack said, "Where would I get the welcoming packet?"

"Not sure," Nick said. "They gave me one the second I arrived. It's definitely piqued my interest. Sounds kinda cool."

"Huh? It does sound cool. Hopefully, I can," Jack said as he stared back into the sea and watched another boat careen across the waters.

"Well, it's either that or the ferry," Nick said. "That one goes in the other direction."

"The ferry?"

"Yeah, that's a longer trip that more people take than you'd imagine. But I see you don't have a red wristband, so it doesn't look like you're on the ferry."

"A red wristband? What's that for?" Jack asked.

"Kinda signifies the group that's going on the ferry versus the boat. If you don't have one, you can't get on the ferry."

"Huh," Jack said once more. He glanced back over to Michael, who was still in conversation with the woman holding the tablet. He looked closely at the woman and noticed she was holding a handful of red wristbands.

He immediately felt a sense of nervousness as he heard Nick say, "Well, nice meeting you. I leave in a few hours. Maybe we'll see you again. Oh, and good luck getting the packet. I think they should have given you one, to be honest, but they do things different here." Nick took a drink from the bartender and started to walk away.

Jack watched him and then looked back over to Michael and the woman and saw the woman point in his direction. Nervously, Jack stood up and called back to Nick, "Hey, Nick! Excuse me."

Nick stopped and turned back. "Yeah?"

"Are you going toward the boat now?" Jack asked.

"I was going to make one stop while I had the time, and then I'm heading down right after," Nick replied.

Jack looked back at the woman with the tablet and studied her handful of red wristbands for a second. Then he turned back to Nick and said, "Do you mind if I join you?"

"Yeah, sure, come on! The place I wanted to check out is supposed to be a blast. You might enjoy it too," Nick said.

Jack nervously looked back over to Michael and the woman. Then, like a child trying to evade a parent's stare, he slid off his barstool, hurried across to Nick, and tried to blend in without being noticed.

As the two men walked away, Michael and the woman looked up in their direction. She closed her tablet and handed Michael one wristband.

Chapter Eleven

Dante's Restaurant

Jack kept on glancing back as Nick walked through the atrium pathway as if he knew exactly where he was going. Jack was a few steps behind and quickened his pace as Nick followed a stamped concrete path lined by tropical foliage. The path led them into a plaza where shops and restaurants filled the space.

As Jack looked around, he was once more overwhelmed by the sight. "What is this place?" he asked.

"Isn't it great? They have everything here," Nick replied. "Any type of restaurant you could think of, and some pretty great clubs if we have some time."

"Wow! This is something," Jack said as they walked through the plaza, passing one ethnic restaurant after another.

Still a few steps behind, Jack quickened his pace to keep up as Nick looked over and said, "Do you want to grab a quick bite? I hear there is an amazing Italian restaurant just ahead with a giant cheese wheel they cook your pasta in."

"Yeah, that sounds great," Jack said.

"Okay, it's right up ahead," Nick said as he led Jack up through the plaza and directly into the area of the Italian restaurant. The restaurant's name was Dante's. "Check it out," Nick said as he stopped in front of the restaurant.

The restaurant was gigantic. It had its own plaza within its entrance where local musicians played Italian music while the patrons entered the bistro.

"This place keeps on getting more amazing every second," Jack said.

Nick walked directly into the restaurant as if he was a regular and sat down at a table near the front. Jack watched as Nick sat, and he tentatively followed him.

The second they sat, three servers came up to them and served them bread, water, and appetizers. Nick looked up at Jack and saw he was perplexed as the servers were so attentive and said, "Oh, there's no ordering here. They just bring it out to you until you're done."

"Really?" Jack replied as he watched them set down an appetizer that resembled a small wooden tree. The base of the tree had burrata cheese, sweet peppers, bruschetta bread, and olives. Prosciutto hung from the tree's branches.

"Will you look at that!" Jack said in amazement.

"Pretty awesome, huh?" Nick replied as he leaned in and peeled a piece of prosciutto off a branch.

"So what's over at the dock?" Jack asked.

Nick leaned back in his chair and said, "I hear it's where there is access to the private island."

"Private island?" Jack asked.

"Well, it's kind of what I'm calling it. Sometimes it's not the easiest ticket to get in."

"Are you talking about heaven?" Jack said.

"Call it whatever you want. But I will tell you, people are dying to get in." Nick started to laugh at his own joke.

"Funny," Jack said cynically. "But the access is at the dock, right?"

"That's my understanding. But you know what, we got some time here," Nick said. "Might as well enjoy it. Do you want some pasta? You gotta see them cook it in the cheese wheel."

"Yeah, sure," Jack replied, confused. He looked around the restaurant as the servers approached. They rolled in a large cart with a gigantic cheese wheel lying on its side. The wheel's center was carved out like a massive bowl as the servers prepared their pasta. As if they were putting on a culinary exhibition, they rolled the already prepared pasta in a pan nearby and tossed it into the base of the cheese wheel.

Once the pasta was in the base of the wheel, they added more olive oil and a shot of whiskey. Flames erupted upward for a moment as Jack sat amazed by the presentation.

"Pretty cool, huh?" Nick said.

"Very cool," Jack replied as the servers twirled the long homemade pasta into two perfectly nested balls and placed them on plates for both men. One of the serving chefs said, "Bon appétit!" as they wrapped up their cart and went on to the next table. They both started to eat while enjoying the Italian music in the plaza.

"So how was your flight over?" Nick asked.

"Pretty interesting. I've never seen anything quite like it."

"Yeah. A little too much for my taste. I thought it was kind of showy, to be honest."

"Too showy?" Jack asked.

"Yeah. I mean, it's like they really want to impress us or something," Nick replied.

"Oh, I didn't get that feeling at all. I just thought it was a kind of a beautiful beginning," Jack said as he ate his pasta.

"Huh ... well, you can call it what you want. I thought it was showy," Nick said.

Nick finished his dish and wiped his mouth. He then pulled out a cigar and said to Jack, "Do you mind?"

"No, help yourself," Jack said as he continued to clean his plate.

Nick smiled at him as he placed the cigar in his mouth and proceeded to fire up a large flame in front of it. The flame lit up his face as he twirled the cigar in an effort to light the entire circumference.

After it was lit, he took a large puff and blew a thick stream of smoke upward. He turned to Jack and said, "I could do this all day."

Jack smiled and replied, "Yeah, it is pretty nice."

"Almost makes me want to think of a way to stay right here. Can't imagine it getting any better."

"That's not what I understand," Jack said. "Apparently, this doesn't hold a candle to Heaven."

"The private island, huh? Yeah, that's what they tell ya. But how can we be so sure?" Nick asked as he took another puff on his cigar.

"I guess that's where our faith comes in, right?"

"I suppose," Nick replied with a quizzical laugh.

"Plus I have someone waiting for me."

"Oh, you do, do ya? And who would that be?"

"My wife," Jack said with confidence.

"Your wife?"

"Yes, absolutely. I know she is."

"Oh, you do?" Nick replied. "Well, I'm not sure who served you that load of you-know-what, but if I were you, I would manage my expectations."

Surprised, Jack said, "How can you say that? How would you know?"

"Hey buddy, I'm a realist. Always been. I'm just telling ya. You better watch what you're wishing for here."

Jack sat back in his chair and thought for a moment. "No, I'm sure she is. I just need to find her, and it sounds like the dock is my entry."

Nick took another puff on his cigar and said, "Maybe so, but not so sure that is a guarantee. But I will tell you though, there's supposed to be a guy who could guarantee all that type of stuff for you here."

"A guy? Here, there's a guy? Really?" Jack said sarcastically.

"Really. First person I ran into when I arrived," Nick declared. "To be honest with you, changed my perspective on everything."

"How so?" Jack asked.

"Opened my eyes to some of the fables we have been fed for years. You know how the media can condition you? Well, we've been conditioned, buddy boy. And let me tell you, it is quite an interesting fable. You call it faith; I call it a smoke screen."

Jack stared at him in disbelief and said, "What are you saying? That God, Jesus, the Holy Spirit—that Heaven isn't real?"

"I'm not saying anything; you are. Maybe you should listen to your own words."

Flustered, Jack replied, "No way! I don't believe that. How do you explain all of this?"

Nick looked around and said, "This? I can't explain any of it. To be honest, I'm not sure any of it is real either."

Completely confused, Jack sat back in his chair and stared off into the plaza as Nick took another puff of his cigar.

After a few moments of uncomfortable silence, Nick got up and said, "You know what, let's go talk to him. I think he's still at the club. He can help you sort all this out. And he may even be able to point you in the right direction for that reunion you are seeking, or even set you up with someone new. That might be fun, huh?"

"Someone new? No way!" Jack said. "Not me! No, Dolly was all I ever wanted and needed. Can't replace someone like that."

"You mean to tell me you never wanted anyone after her?"

"Yeah, honest to God. When I lost her, I lost half of me. I never could or even wanted to replace her. Believe me, in my case it was incomprehensible to replace something so perfect in my life. Never even wanted to try. Hey, what can I tell you? I'm a simple type of guy. She was and will always be then only one for me. That's it, end of story."

Nick listened to him with his eyebrow raised and said, "Whatever! Sounds like a limited story to me, but I guess we're all different, huh?"

"Yeah, I guess we are. And you know what? I'm good with that. You can call me what you want, but when it comes down to my heart and soul, Dolly is the only one. So tell me more about this guy of yours. Can he really help me with finding her?" Jack said with renewed interest.

"If anyone can, this guy can," Nick said as he pointed to himself.

Jack thought for a moment about his gesture and said, "All right, then, yeah. Let's go."

Chapter Twelve

The Turning Point Lounge

Jack got up and followed Nick out of the restaurant and back into the plaza. The marketplace was filling up with more people heading to the various restaurants as Nick led Jack. They passed kiosks and smaller street-type vendors as Jack marveled at the activity.

"There seems to be more people than before," Jack said.

"Yeah, it's a pretty steady stream here," Nick replied. "This place is always busy. Kinda helps separate the boat and the ferry people too."

"Really?" Jack said in a confused manner.

"Yeah, at least that's what they tell me," Nick said.

"Huh?" Jack said, following Nick as he made his way down the plaza path toward a club named The Turning Point at the end of the strip. The club featured a piano bar with music spilling into the streets. A crowd of patrons sat and stood near the open outdoor pavilion setting while they enjoyed the single entertainer on the piano belting out seventies and eighties classic rock tunes.

As they strolled up to the bar, Jack's ear perked up when he heard the classic Journey song "Don't Stop Believing" coming from inside.

"I love this song!" Jack exclaimed as they walked up to the outside perimeter of the bar to watch the piano man entertain the crowd.

Nick strolled up, and swung his leg around an open-back barstool, and sat down. "Yeah, it's not bad. There's better, though."

He quickly got up from his stool and walked near the piano man. He grabbed a small piece of paper on the bar and wrote on it. Once finished he folded the paper and placed it in a request jar near the piano. He strolled back to the barstool and sat down.

"'Not bad'? You're crazy! This is a classic," Jack said as he too pulled up a barstool and sat.

"We can agree to disagree, I suppose. I have a better one coming," Nick said as they both turned and listened to the entertainer. As the piano man sang the song, Jack absorbed the environment and soaked in the tune, saying, "Man, I love live music. Really, nothing is better."

"I can agree on that one," Nick replied as they both bobbed their heads to the chorus of the song.

Midway through the tune, Nick turned back to Jack and said, "So I can't believe you never remarried or anything. That just sounds nuts to me."

"What can I tell ya? I was blessed," Jack said. "When you find that one person who fits you like the perfect glove, you can never replace it. Nor do you want to. We were truly made for each other. I can't wait to see her again."

"Again? Remember, manage those expectations," Nick replied.

"Why do you keep saying that?" Jack snapped back. "I believe that with all my heart. I don't care what you think; I'm going to find her."

"I'm just saying, I never put all my eggs in one basket. This way, I'm never disappointed. Whatever the outcome is, I'm good with it."

"Well, we are different there. How about you? Were you ever married?" Jack asked.

"Married? Ha! Sure, a few times. But believe me, you won't find me searching for them here. I'm free, and I'm enjoying. You should too!" Nick exclaimed as he looked over to a pair of sexy women near the piano bar.

Jack also looked over at the women by the bar and said, "No, thanks. I'm good."

"Wasteful way of thinking, my friend," Nick replied as the piano man neared the finish of the Journey song.

"So where is this guy of yours?" Jack asked.

"Oh, he's around," Nick said as he kept on staring at the women at the bar.

Jack turned from Nick and surveyed the crowd in the bar as the music played. He noticed that most of the patrons were wearing the red wristband.

Concerned, he looked back over to Nick and said, "How did you hear about this place?"

"It's one of my favorites," Nick said.

"It's one of your favorites? How long did you say you've been here?" Jack asked, a bit uneasy.

Nick ignored him as he made eye contact with the women at the bar. The piano man finished his song and said, "Welcome, all newcomers to The Turning Point lounge. You've finally made it to the place where all your dreams come true. Tonight, we are playing requests only. Come on up, pop your request in the jar, and your tune will be on in no time at all. Let's see what we got next."

The piano man reached into the jar and pulled out Nick's request saying, "Okay, here we go. This is a request from a longtime patron." The piano man looked over to Nick and said, "This one is for you, old friend."

Jack peered at Nick and said, "Old friend?" Nick smiled in a sly manner over to the piano man and the women by the bar. He placed his cigar once more in his mouth and fired up the flame to light it.

The piano man hit the keys on his board and played. As the music started, Jack immediately felt a sickening feeling in his stomach as the piano man sang, "Please allow me to introduce myself, I'm a man of wealth and taste. I've been around for long, long years, stole million man's soul an' faith. And I was 'round when Jesus Christ had his moment of doubt and pain. Made damn sure that Pilate washed his hands and sealed his fate. Pleased to meet you; hope you guess my name. But what's puzzling you is the nature of my game."

Jack looked over to Nick, with his lit cigar, now flanked by the two women. Nick turned to Jack with a sinister look and held up the red wristband. "You wanna see her? Put it on."

The pain in Jack's stomach increased as he realized he was not talking to any ordinary man. He immediately fell back and staggered off his barstool to move away from Nick and said, "No—no. You, get away! God, please help me."

Nick looked at him calmly with a woman now on each arm and said, "Keep it simple, Jack. Don't buy into all the other hype. They don't exist. I told you that. It's all a lie. If you want to see her, I'll get her for you. Now put the band on." He reached out to hand Jack the red wristband.

The sickening feeling increased within the pit of his stomach as Jack kept on backing up away from them as the rest of the bar created a circle around him. "No, no—you get away from me!"

"All you have to do is put it on, my friend. Everything will be taken care of," Nick said, laughing as the crowd increased to circle him.

The piano man continued and sang directly toward Jack, "Pleased to meet you; hope you guess my name, Jackie boy. Oh yeah! But what's puzzling you is the nature of my game."

Jack looked around and felt the crowd circling in on him more as he continued to step away. "No! You leave me alone. God, please help me!"

"Stop it, Jack! I can give you all you seek," Nick said. "Just let go, give in to me. It will all be okay."

"Dear Jesus, please help me!" Jack blurted out as he was able to break free from the circle of patrons around him. The circle opened as if his words of prayer had split them apart to make a pathway of escape. As Jack turned and saw an opening, he quickly took off and scampered out of the piano bar.

Nick immediately got a cynical and frustrated look on his face. He took the red wristband, threw it on the ground and said, "Damn!"

The piano man kept on playing the tune as Jack successfully escaped the bar.

As he stumbled and scampered his way out of the plaza, he ran as fast as he could. While he ran, he once more felt the aches and pains of his body returning. His legs felt weighted down as if he were running under water. His stomach hurt, and his cough came back with a vengeance.

He saw the end of the plaza about fifty yards ahead, and it took all his energy to pass by each restaurant, kiosk, and street vendor. Just as he was going to make it to the end of the marketplace, he noticed a white light near the exit. He also saw and felt the dark mist, which had come back and hovered around him.

The warmth of the white light drew him in, and he felt calmer with each step he took toward it. His body still ached uncontrollably, and his cough was out of control at this stage, but the light felt incredible all the same.

Just as he was going to make it out of the plaza, he noticed a man standing near the light. As he came closer to pass by, the man's face became visible. Jack immediately stopped and focused on the man, who stood a little over five feet tall, with Middle Eastern skin tones, dark hair, and a full beard.

A sense of relief came over him like none other before. He stared at the man with the light shining around him. Within seconds, his cough interrupted him and the pains within his body increased.

The man with the Middle Eastern skin tones, dark hair, and a full beard simply looked at Jack with a reassuring smile. Jack felt a sense of calmness within his soul as he instantly closed his eyes and fell to the street. The dark mist now fully encircled him.

Jack was back in his bedroom, surrounded by his three kids and close six-pack friends.

Chapter Thirteen

Reminiscing

With his eyes still shut, Jack lay in his bed and felt the presence of many people around him. To open his eyes took more than he could manage, but nonetheless, he could feel who was in the room with him.

He heard every conversation and responded to each request within his own psyche. As grandchildren, close friends, and his kids spoke to him, Jack communicated, but his dialogue was more cerebral than outward.

His only challenge was that he knew deep down they could not hear him. but somehow it was okay. Even though they spoke and sometimes screamed out his name to gain a reaction, Jack had a unique comfort of interaction that made his experience more tolerable.

As the hours drifted and the presence of more loved ones entering the room filled his being, Jack listened as stories of his and Dolly's past circulated within the room. He first heard his daughter, Annie as she said, "Do you guys remember the vacation we took to Vegas?"

"Oh my God," Jack Jr. said, "I still can't believe we went to Vegas of all places as a family."

"Well, that's because the prices were so good, and we were able to use the time-share to get the suites," Lily added.

"Suites? Not sure it was that sweet," Danny replied. "I had to sleep on two chairs the whole trip."

"That's because you fit," Jack Jr. said.

"Yeah, you would've fit too," Danny said.

"Guess it was a seniority thing. You didn't complain though," Jack Jr. said.

"Who would've listened? It's the curse of the third child," Danny said. They all laughed as Danny smirked.

Lily jumped in again and said, "How about your mother in the pool?"

"Oh my God, to this day I still laugh about that," Annie replied.

"What happened in the pool?" another member of the six-pack blurted out.

Lily got up and moved closer to Jack and the bed as the rest of the group sat around and listened. "It was classic Dolly. Remember, it was Vegas, and we decided to bring the kids, who at the time ranged from eight to probably fifteen. Probably wasn't the greatest idea, but we traveled so well together, it really didn't matter where we went. Anyway, we're at the pool one day, and everyone is having a great time. The kids are swimming and ordering their chicken fingers every minute they can, and suddenly we see Dolly get into the pool and scream, 'It's aerobic time!'"

"Oh, no way!" one of the six-pack said.

"I swear to God. She entered the pool like she was the instructor from the gym and started her own class. First it was just us in the pool. And she kept on screaming her instructions, and slowly but surely more guests from the pool joined in. It was hilarious! Within ten minutes, she had half the pool doing aerobics as she would scream out, 'Okay, ladies … move your jugs, move your jugs.' By the time she finished, she had guests coming up to her asking when the next class was. It was great. And the Vegas crowd loved it more than you know."

The room laughed as they all remembered the story and how Dolly could walk into a room and take it over. With his eyes still shut tightly, Jack absorbed the entire story and felt a warm feeling of remembrance as Lily finished up.

"That was something else," Annie said. "That's how she was, though. She could walk into any situation like that and comfortably set everyone to enjoying themselves. She had such a way about herself that people welcomed, even if she was in your face."

"What about the time you guys went to Napa and you had the mud baths?" Danny asked.

"Oh my God, that's another one," Lily said. "Your father was the funny one on that one."

"Tell us that story, Aunt Lily," Annie said. "The kids love to hear stories about their Papa and Gram Gram. Right, kids?"

The grandchildren sat up to listen.

"Okay," Lily began. "Well, your father and I aren't brother and sister, but clearly could have been. Same interests, same bad habits, and same adventuresome spirit. Anyway, we were going to Napa, and instead of the normal type of spa, we were both interested in doing something different. Somehow, we heard about the mud treatment at this very unique spa which featured an experience involving volcanic ash."

"Volcanic ash?" Danny asked.

"Yes, Apparently the site was on some old volcano. So we go to the spa because your father and I convince your mother and Uncle Sal. They were accepting and willing troupers, those two."

"Accepting, I don't think so," Uncle Sal said cynically.

"Oh, yes you were. Just listen. Anyway, we pull up to this spa, which is set in some 1960s motif, and proceed to go into the bath area. They separated male and female and ask us to disrobe. We were asked to walk naked into this room that had concrete-like coffins on the floor. We then were to climb into the concrete coffins which had a layer of hot volcanic mud in the bottom. As soon as we were securely in, the staff from the spa shoveled layer after layer of hot mud on top of us."

"How hot was it?" Jack Jr. asked.

"Oh, it was hot, believe me," Uncle Sal said. "We sat in that mud for about ten minutes, and I could tell your father was starting to feel it already. Remember, we were in Napa drinking all night before."

"Ah—who is telling this story, Sal?" Lily said.

"Go ahead, just filling in spots," Sal said as the kids laughed at the two of them bickering.

"Filling in spots, are you? So where was I?" Lily asked.

"The mud in the concrete-like coffins," Danny said.

"Thank you, Danny. After the mud, they told us to shower, and oh, my dear Jesus, it took a while to get that mud off. I think I found mud in spots I didn't know I had for days later. Anyway, we did not have much time because they told us to go into a hot tub next."

"Oh, let me tell this part," Sal exclaimed. "You weren't with us for this one."

"Sure, my sweet pea, you go right ahead," Lily sarcastically said.

"So your father and I go next into this hot tub. They were two separate bathtubs with scalding water, and when I say scalding, they were boiling hot. We both submerged ourselves in the tubs, and within seconds I look over to him and his head is drooped over. I could tell he was hurting. Sweat was beginning to pour from his head, and he kept trying to raise his body above the water to try and cool off. I was feeling it too, but he was hurting from the night before.

"We finally were able to get out of this hot boiling soup of tub water, and the next phase was a tiny sauna the size of a small shower. We go into this thing with towels wrapped around us, and there is only one small bench. Your father immediately sits on the bench as the heat from the sauna rises. There was this tiny hole in the sauna that led to outside. It only took seconds for your dad to find the hole in the wall as he stuck his nose and face on it to suck in the outside air. Like two scuba divers with only one small oxygen mask, we took turns putting our face on the hole in the wall to get any form of relief. It was brutal but hilarious at the same time. All of this, because these two knuckleheads wanted a different type of spa experience."

The kids and the rest of the room laughed as Sal finished his story.

"Oh my God that is so great," Annie said. "I love these old stories."

"They are great, and there are so many more. That's just the tip," Lily said.

The room loosened up now and continued with more stories of both Jack and Dolly as Jack absorbed his surroundings the best he could.

After a few more stories, Jack could feel the calm within his spirit once more as he drifted away into a cradled slumber.

Chapter Fourteen

The Dinghy

Jack awoke to find himself sitting on a pier near a white sand beach. As he looked around, he could see the resort he had come from as well as the plaza nearby. The gigantic umbrella holm oak tree provided a familiar landmark as he took in the solitude of the moment and said, "Okay … now what?"

He sat on the pier for a few moments and finally decided to get up and walk the beach. The crystal turquoise blue water was uncommonly clear and calm. As far as he could see the ocean in front of him resembled more of an indoor pool than a large body of sea water. It was breathtaking as he strolled barefoot through the water and white sand below.

After a few minutes of strolling aimlessly, he stopped to soak in the solitude. Ankle-deep in the crystal blue water, he stood on the beach as the gentle tide rolled up and over his feet repeatedly. He took in a deep breath and felt the serenity of the environment within his soul. The peaceful, easy feeling rushed through his being like an injection of calmness.

He closed his eyes and felt the water roll back and forth over his ankles. He took in one more deep breath and opened his eyes to stare out into the surreal ocean in front of him. After a few seconds more of solitude, he heard an engine. He looked around to see where this sound was coming from, and in the distance, he could see a tiny inflatable dinghy raft coming toward him.

Curious, he watched as the dinghy floated directly toward him, driven by a young man of Jamaican descent. The man piloting the raft had long dark braided hair with cornrows and beads flowing downward.

Jack stood in the water and waited as the boat floated right up to him. The man in the boat said, "Hello, Jackie boy. How are you doing today, mon?"

Confused, Jack looked up at the man and said, "Do I know you?"

"Oh, probably not, mon. My name is Abisai and I am your ride."

"My ride?" Jack asked.

"Yeah, mon, time to go over to the boat," Abisai said.

"The boat? Not the ferry, right?" Jack asked.

"Oh no, not the ferry, mon," Abisai replied; "that be going in the other direction."

"You sure about that? How do I know you're not tricking me like the last guy?" Jack said.

"No trick here, mon. You're protected. You've always been," Abisai said.

"Protected? How so?"

"You accepted him, mon."

"Accepted him?" Jack said.

"John 3:16, mon. As long as you believe in him, you're golden."

"Then what about the ferry and that Nick guy?"

"Some spirits just don't give up here, mon. They'll try to the end. No worries though, you've got that protection. You ready to go?"

"Ah—yeah," Jack said. "So where are we going?"

"I'm taking you first over to the weigh station. The boat will take you from there."

"The weigh station?"

"Yeah, mon. You're almost there," Abisai said. "Just a little more patience."

Jack looked around the beach and took in the serenity once more as he turned back to Abisai and said in agreement, "Okay, let's do this."

"All right, mon, come along," Abisai said with a beckoning gesture.

Jack swung his leg over the side of the inflatable dinghy and climbed aboard.

"Let's go!" Abisai said as they drove off into the sea.

Chapter Fifteen

The Weigh Station

Abisai navigated the dingy across the serene turquoise blue water as if they were gliding on glass. The water below barely rippled as the calmness and tranquility of the ride provided a soothing transport toward the weigh station.

As they floated along, Jack occasionally dipped his cupped hand into the water, allowing for the gentle flow and spray of the warm sea against his welcoming appendage. The gentle splash and occasional ripple provided almost a therapeutic massage as Jack lost himself in the aquatic transport nearing the station.

The dinghy floated up and onto the beach as its base rubbed against the coastline and came to a stop on top of the pure white sand. As the craft rested, Jack noticed more dinghies approaching the shoreline and weigh station. One by one, they all floated smoothly up and onto the beach.

"We're here, Jackie boy!" Abisai said.

Jack looked up and saw a gigantic tiki hut about two hundred yards away. He swung his legs off the dinghy and splashed his feet into the ankle-deep water below. "So what is this place?"

"It's the weigh station, mon," Abisai replied.

Jack watched as the other dinghies approached and dropped off other passengers and said, "What happens at the weigh station?"

"It's where you get weighed, mon," Abisai said with a smile.

Jack looked up at the gigantic tiki hut and said, "You can't be serious!"

"Yeah, mon. The spirit is like a feather; need to make sure you're not carrying any excess weight on you in order to soar."

"Excess weight? Soar?"

"Yeah, mon. Believe me, a lot of excess baggage is accumulated by people over the years. It just weighs you down, mon. It's important to shed all that excess before you get on the boat."

"You are serious. How do I know if I'm overweight or not?" Jack asked.

"That's why we're at the weigh station, mon."

"Is that right?" Jack said as they both got out of the boat and walked toward the gigantic tiki structure.

While walking up, Jack saw the other passengers making their individual treks up toward the hut, and he also saw at the other end of the coastline a large ferry approaching the shore.

He stopped and hesitantly said, "Hey, wait a second. I thought this was where we would pick up the boat. That looks like a ferry to me."

"That's because that is a ferry, mon," Abisai replied. "Not yours though; you pick up the boat on the other side."

"Then why is that here?"

"Aw, mon, even if you're on the ferry, you always still get that last-minute opportunity to shed the wristband. People just need to take it, mon. Unfortunately, many don't."

"Huh?" Jack said, following Abisai as they headed to the hut.

As they reached the structure and walked inside, a perplexed Jack looked around and saw nothing inside other than four small nightstands standing here and there in the hut. The inside resembled an indoor field house with nothing but finely cut grass within its circumference.

The nightstands each had a book propped on them and were spread out at various locations in the hut. Jack noticed each of the stands and then looked around at the passengers from the dinghy. He did a quick count and came up with a total of four people including himself walking into the hut.

As he made it closer to one of the stands, he saw the book which was propped upright on top, and it was the same book Michael was reading the plane, *When You Get There*. Each book was also personalized to the passenger arriving.

The first book was for Abba. Jack saw the name and then watched as a man in his mid-eighties with gray hair and a beard walked up to the stand to retrieve it. Curious, Jack made his way to the next nightstand. This one was designated to Yeshua. He watched as the same bearded young Middle-Eastern-looking man he had seen earlier walked up to the stand.

Perplexed and slightly concerned his name was not on either one of them, Jack continued to the next stand. This one was designated to Paraclete. Before Jack knew it, a woman with a Swedish appearance and in her mid-twenties approached the stand and said, "There you are." She strolled past Jack as if she were floating on air and picked up the book.

Jack looked at all three of them and said to Abisai, "Wait a second, that's not—?"

"Pretty cool, eh, mon?" Abisai replied.

"No way! Abba, the Father; Yeshua, the Son; and Paraclete, I'm guessing, the Holy Spirit. Right? They're three distinct people?" Jack said.

"You know, mon, it's a better way to understand him or them

individually," Abisai said. "If not, it would be too much for you to comprehend right now. Breaking them in three may help you better appreciate your time with them."

"Are they here, just for me?" Jack asked.

"They're here for everyone, Jack. This just happens to be closer to your moment. But, yes, they are here for you."

"My moment?"

"Why don't you go get the book?" Abisai said, pointing to the final nightstand.

Jack nervously turned toward the stand and gingerly started toward it. As he got closer, he couldn't make out the title due to how the book was turned on the stand. Slowly speeding up, he ended in a jogging sprint to the nightstand.

As he got there, he rushed around to see the featured name on the book, and to his utter and complete relief, it said Jack Mandisa. "Oh, thank God!" He said as he reached down and grabbed the book off the nightstand.

He stared at the cover as he read his name on it next to the title *When You Get There*.

"Wow!" He took the book in both hands and readied to open it. With a deep breath, he slowly cracked opened the binder to gaze at the pages within.

Dumbfounded, he looked at the pages and said, "What is this?"

All the pages within the book were blank. He also noticed as Abba, Yeshua, and Paraclete tucked their individual books away and walked out of the hut.

Abisai walked up to him, pointed to the title of the book, and said, "When *you* get there, mon."

"What do you mean when I get there? Am I not here?" Jack said in frustration. "Where is here, and more importantly, where is there? And when do I get there?"

"Soon, mon," Abisai said, "you're close. Just a little more patience."

"A little more patience. A little more?" Jack said.

"A little more, Jackie. Now, take your book and follow them. I may see you in a little bit, but you need to go that way now. I know you have questions." Abisai pointed to the other three who were now walking out of the hut and into an area of tropical jungle.

"I do have questions, and you're not coming?" Jack replied.

"I was just your ride, mon. You go ahead now. Remember, you are protected. Now go!"

Jack looked up at the exit and then back to Abisai. "I'm protected, huh?"

"Always have been. But it does help to reinforce it every now and then," Abisai said and then gestured the sign of the cross with a slight smile and said, "See ya, mon."

Jack shook his hand and said, "See ya, mon." He laughed as he turned and followed the others out of the hut and onto a path which led into the jungle.

Chapter Sixteen

The Path

Jack followed Abba, Yeshua, and Paraclete through the path. On each side of them, tropical foliage engulfed their surroundings. The jungle-like atmosphere provided zero visibility within the foliage, but the dirt path in front of them was carved out to perfection.

The winding trek made for a visual array of tropical views along the way. On both sides of the path, waterfalls, and stunning rock formations set into the landscape made for a gorgeous walk through the jungle.

Jack marveled at the site of the falls and the rocks as they continued along the path.

"Excuse me. Are we going to walk for a while?" Jack asked.

Abba, who was leading the group, turned back and said, "The path ultimately has its end, my wayward son. For now, you are to carry on."

"It's not that far, bud," Yeshua said to Jack, patting him on the back as he passed him as if they had been best friends for years.

"It is quite beautiful, though," Paraclete, said. "I wonder if we have time to stop and take it in." She whisked past him to admire one of the numerous waterfalls along the way.

Jack, who was now behind all of them, moved up beside Paraclete, who had now stopped to admire the falls. Abba and Yeshua continued down the path. He slowed for a bit and said, "I—uh—don't think we should stop here, right? They never told us to stop on the path."

Paraclete kept on staring at the falls and said, "They never told us not to, sweetie."

As Jack walked past her, he could not help but notice the amazing sight of the waterfall she was admiring. It was simply breathtaking as he gingerly made his way around her.

"I'm not sure, but I think we need to keep moving, though, to catch up to the others," he said.

"Suit yourself. I'm going to take it in for a bit," Paraclete said as she took a step off the path toward the falls nearby.

Concerned, Jack stopped and turned toward her and said, "I'm not sure you should."

"It's okay, sweetie. I'm all grown up," Paraclete replied as she continued steadily on her way.

Perplexed, Jack looked ahead as the others kept on walking. "Hey wait!" He rushed up toward the other two and said, "Should we wait for her?"

Abba turned around and said, "Waiting may take longer than you may desire."

"Yeah, but are we supposed to leave her?" Jack said.

"Let your heart guide you, son," Abba said as he turned and kept to the path.

Jack turned to Yeshua and said, "What do you think?"

Yeshua looked at Abba as he kept to the path and said, "The heart—oh, let that thing guide you, buddy boy."

Yeshua turned and continued along the path as Jack stood in a perplexed state. He watched them walk away and then turned back toward the falls. He saw Paraclete walked toward it.

After a few seconds of contemplation, he shook his head and said, "I think I have to." He turned toward the waterfall and stepped off the path to head toward Paraclete.

Chapter Seventeen

The Falls

The waterfall was just a hundred yards away as Jack cautiously walked through the rock-filled water below his feet. The stream leading up to the falls was shin-deep as he trekked through to get closer to Paraclete, who was now sitting on a larger boulder near the falls.

As he got closer, she looked up and said, "Isn't it beautiful?"

Jack gazed at the falls and said, "Yeah, it really is."

"You didn't have to come back for me," she said. "I would have eventually made it up to you."

"Yeah—well, something told me not to leave you alone out here. But I think we should be getting back," Jack replied.

"Why in such a hurry? Don't you want to take in this beauty?" she said.

"Sure, but I'm trying to get to the boat, and I really don't want to waste too much time or jeopardize my chances of going."

"It's always about time, isn't it?" Paraclete said. "And jeopardize your chance'? Boy, you are a worrier, aren't you?"

"Not really a worrier. I'm just concerned about missing it."

"Not a worrier, huh?" Paraclete said, turning back to the falls.

"I guess I am a little bit impatient," Jack said.

"You know, if you look closely at the droplets, you can see all kinds of wondrous things."

"Is that right?" Jack said as he stared at the falls for a few moments. Awkwardly, Paraclete did not say much. She took in the beauty of the nature surrounding them and seemed to be absorbing every aspect of it.

Growing impatient, Jack said, "Okay, I guess I'm going to go back then," as he slowly turned away from her.

"Why is the boat so important to you?" Paraclete asked.

"It's not the boat, it's what it can bring me to," Jack replied.

"Dolly?" Paraclete said as she turned toward him.

Jack stopped in his tracks and said, "How do you know her name?"

"All of us know Dolly. We know you too, Jack," Paraclete said as the waterfall mist sprayed upward behind her.

"Who are you?" Jack asked.

"Let's just say, I am," she replied. "We are all here to help you along on the last leg."

"Last leg? I don't understand."

"We're here to assist, during the final transition."

"The final transition?" Jack asked.

"You're getting closer, Jack."

"So, I am going to get on the boat soon?"

"Back to worrying again, huh?" she said.

"I'm not worrying, I'm—"

Paraclete interrupted him and replied, "Take a look." She motioned her hand toward the mist within the waterfall.

As Jack looked up, he saw images of Dolly and his kids when they were younger around the Christmas tree. "What's this?" Jack said.

"Just a little recap." Paraclete said as they both watched the images recap various events in Jack and Dolly's life.

Within a few seconds, Jack found himself enjoying the review as he also settled onto a boulder. The images recapped their holidays, birthdays, and special happenings through the years. Sprinkled within the images, snippets of videos also emerged as, for the first time in years, Jack heard Dolly's voice again.

He was completely taken aback as he heard her comment on a Christmas gift from years ago. "Oh, I remember this like it was yesterday." He relaxed and enjoyed the next set of events being displayed.

"Let's go, people. We're running late," Jack heard his own voice from the video playing.

"Do you remember this one?" Paraclete said as she watched the scene unfold.

Jack watched, saying, "What's this? I don't remember filming this."

Paraclete looked over to him. "Who said anything thing about filming? This is coming from you, Jack."

"Me?" he said.

"I'm not the one projecting these memories; this is all you. Maybe it's something you want to discuss and get rid of."

"I don't understand."

"Let's watch," she said as the video continued in the mist of the waterfall.

"Dad, it's Christmas morning, can't we relax a bit," a ten-year-old Annie said.

"Relax? Relax! You know there's no relaxing on Christmas. We have two more places to go before we're back home for all the people to get here," Jack replied.

"Dad, it's only eight-thirty a.m.," Annie said.

"Exactly, we're running late. Now, let's get cleaned up and get moving," Jack said, as the kids were all in midstream, still opening their presents.

"Aw, honey, can't we just take a few minutes to enjoy this?" Dolly said to Jack.

"Are you kidding me? You know as well as I do how important it is we hit our time slots. If we don't, we'll be late for breakfast at your parents' and the brunch at mine. Not to mention, we have everyone coming back here by three thirty. No, we gotta go!" Jack exclaimed as he walked around the room pulling the paper off the kids' presents and throwing it in the garbage bag to clean up.

"I don't want to go, Daddy!" four-year-old Danny screamed.

"Me either, I want to play with my Nintendo," six-year-old Jack Jr. said.

"Well, we can play later. Now we're getting cleaned up to go to breakfast at your grandparents'," Jack said as he picked up Danny and a few more papers to throw away.

Danny cried out once more as he cried out, "I don't want to go!"

"I don't want to go!" Jack Jr. screamed.

"Neither do I, Dad," Annie said.

"We're going now!" Jack shouted at his family as Danny cried in his arms.

"Okay, okay, okay, stop this!" Jack said as he stood up from the boulder in front of the waterfall.

Paraclete looked over to him as the video image within the mist stopped. "That's how you celebrated Christmas?"

"Well, not always," Jack said.

"Must have been on your mind though for it to be projected."

"Our holidays were a bit hectic at times."

"Did you make your time slot schedule?" Paraclete asked.

"Actually, every year," Jack said, a bit ashamed.

"Was it worth it?"

"Well, it's not that it wasn't, because we did enjoy ourselves at both grandparents' houses, but when I see my demeanor like that—Oh my Lord, how much do I regret that behavior?"

"Didn't seem like the best way to approach it or appreciate the day for what it truly was," Paraclete said.

"No, I don't think so. You know, it wasn't that I was intentionally making them miserable on Christmas morning, I just wanted them to have the best day possible while also not disappointing our parents. There was a lot of juggling on those days. I guess it was a lot to throw at kids or anyone on a Christmas morning."

"And was it only about the presents or your time schedule on Christmas for your family?"

"Well, they were a pretty big part of it," Jack said.

"When did you go to church?"

"Oh, that's a whole other one. Church was on Christmas Eve, followed by the same family stops afterward."

"Did the kids appreciate church?" Paraclete asked.

"To be honest, they and probably all of us went through the motions. Something I'm not too proud of, but we did go every year."

"Sadly, you and your family were one of the better ones. Most don't even attend on Christmas, let alone the rest of the year. I think the true meaning is lost for most."

"We can agree on that one," Jack said. "Believe me, I do regret acting like that on holidays. I think we all need a dose of the true meaning to allow us all to cherish the best gift of all. We get lost in all of the other stuff to really appreciate it. I'm truly sorry for that. I know that now, I just wish my young self could have appreciated it more."

"Well, that's the beauty of it all Jack. Age has nothing to do with it. It's understanding the true meaning of not only holidays but our dear Father and his sacrifices for you and allowing yourself to embody it.

Even though you acted like a time-crazed enthusiast all those years ago, you did manage to instill a strong sense of family with all your kids."

As Paraclete continued to speak to him, images of his kids appeared in the mist of the waterfall. The images showed them growing up and becoming parents of their own.

"Both you and Dolly can be proud of who they became. They truly are products of the two of you, and each one of them has instilled the same sense of family you and Dolly implanted so many years ago."

Jack watched the images of his family growing up. He saw them each grow into amazing adults as well as terrific parents. He smiled as the images concluded up into his current existence and said, "Thank you for this. I think I really needed it."

Paraclete looked at him with a smile and said, "Why don't you go and catch up with the others? I don't want you to miss your time schedule on the boat."

"Funny, you're funny," he said as he stood up from the boulder.

"Go on, Jackie. It was so nice to share with you," Paraclete said.

"You sure you're not going to come?"

"I'm good," she said.

"Okay. Thank, thank you!" Jack said as he turned and walked the stream back toward the path.

Chapter Eighteen

A Walk with Jesus

Jack walked for a few minutes along the path until he got to a break in the foliage. The opening provided a view toward the coastline as he stopped to notice the ferry which had been docked by the pier.

He marveled at the number of people who were boarding the craft. The ship was much larger than he had imagined as passenger after passenger loaded on. He was far enough away to appreciate the size of the craft while also remaining securely on the path to avoid any lure to join.

Then he noticed Nick near the pier checking in passengers. Nick saw him on the path and turned to him with his arms stretched out. "There is still time, Jackie boy," he called. "We have plenty of room."

Jack turned quickly away from him and set forth along the path. *You're protected, Jack. Stay the course.* A few steps later, he heard, "You are most definitely protected. I can assure you of it. But watch that one; he won't stop until the end."

Jack looked up and saw Yeshua (Jesus) standing on the path. He then looked back at the ferry and said, "There are so many who are getting on. I can't imagine that's good."

"It breaks my heart, every soul that steps on that craft," Jesus said. "But they all have time to change; some just take a little bit longer."

"Where is …?" Jack said as he looked around for Abba.

"He went ahead," Jesus answered.

"And you, are you … are you Jesus?"

Jesus looked at him and said as if they were old friends, "I am."

Amazed and completely humbled, Jack stared at him, bathed in pure joy, as Jesus started to walk the path. Jack quickly took one more glance at the ferry and hustled to catch up as they left the area while passengers continued to load.

"Where are we going?" Jack asked as he caught up to Jesus.

"I thought you wanted to go to the boat," Jesus said.

Jack slowed for a moment and said, "Ah … am I supposed to want to go on the boat? I think I'm supposed to, right?"

Jesus looked over to him and lightly said, "It's one way of getting there."

"There are others?" Jack asked.

"There are many ways. The boat is quite scenic, though," Jesus replied. "It's really your choice in the end."

"Then why was the boat such a big deal?" Jack said.

"Who told you about the boat in the first place?" Jesus replied.

Jack stopped and realized, "It was Nick, wasn't it?"

"He's a crafty one, that one," Jesus responded.

"So I don't have to rush for any boat?" Jack asked.

"Jack, you don't have to rush for anything."

"I can't believe I bought into all of that. What do I do now then?"

"What is it you want to do?" Jesus said.

Jack stopped and said, "I still want to get there. I still want to see her."

"I know you do. And so does she."

"She does? How do you know that? Oh wait, of course you would know that. Can I talk to her now? Please, can I see her now!"

"Soon, I promise," Jesus said as he turned and stared into Jack's eyes with his crystal blue eyes penetrating.

As Jack stared into his eyes, he suddenly felt a strong emotion and said, "Why, Jesus? Why did you take her so early?"

"Early?" Jesus said.

"Yes, she was in her early fifties. It was so unfair. We were robbed of our time together. I still can't believe it to this day," Jack said, growing even more emotional.

"Who said anything about robbing you of your time together?" Jesus said as they came toward the end of the path. The path opened into what looked like a campground. Abba (God) stood in the center of the campground waiting for them to enter.

"I did. My family and I had to endure all those years without her. It's just not fair," Jack continued.

"What about what is to come? Did you ever calculate eternity versus the time you shared?" Jesus asked.

"Eternity?"

"Yes."

"Um—no, but I guess it's just been so hard without her," Jack said. "She was my everything, and you just took her away."

"Is she really away, Jack?" Jesus replied.

"I—I don't suppose so, but she was. And it was brutal. I just don't understand why she had to go!"

Jesus rested his arm on Jack's shoulder and said, "I assure you, my son, she is not gone."

"So I will see her?" Jack asked again.

Jesus grasped his shoulders and said, "You will see and be with her for eternity."

Jack felt a rush through his body unlike anything he had ever felt before. He looked across to the center of the campground where God stood. God looked up at him and stared at him with the kind of reassuring look only a loving father could deliver and said, "My son, you have done well, my good and faithful servant. Come forth."

At that moment, the black mist appeared once more near Jack as he suddenly felt a rush of pain throughout his body. His hands, arms, and legs ached like nothing before, and his cough was back with a vengeance.

He tried to walk forward, but his legs weakened, and he began to slump to the ground. Within seconds, God, Jesus, Paraclete, Abisai, and Michael all appeared and rushed over to him to assist as he fell into their arms. The black mist surrounded them all.

Jesus said, "It's okay, Jack. Let it go; let it go. Let the transition complete."

Jack stared into Jesus's eyes, and although he felt incredible pain and suffering, he had a comfort unlike anything he had ever felt before. He closed his eyes and reopened them to find himself back in his bedroom with his entire family encircling him.

Chapter Nineteen

Transition

His heartbeat raced as all his family and friends surrounded him. His extended time the past few weeks had clearly taken a toll on the family. It was dusk outside, and his three kids sat in chairs around him as his close family and six-pack friends were saying goodbye for the evening. They, too, had a worn look, as almost everyone in the room had taken turns supporting Jack and the kids over the months leading up to today.

Lily and Sal were the first to leave for the night as they each said goodbye to the kids and then finally Jack, knowing very well, each time they said goodbye now, it could most definitely mean more than it did yesterday.

They each told Jack it was okay to go as they hugged and kissed the kids for the night. Other six-pack friends and close family members followed suit as the room dwindled down to Jack's kids and a few of his grandchildren.

Every now and then one of the kids would come up to him and remind him that it was "okay to go" and that they would be all right. As the night sky crept close, his heart raced even faster. Each kid came back to his bedside and mindlessly stared. This same routine had now been conditioned in them over the past weeks and had become a numbing exercise of surrealism.

Helpless and completely drained, all they could do was glance over at the mere shell he had become. With every intention to remain alert, Annie, Jack Jr., and Danny fought hard to keep watch while uttering phrases of encouragement until all three of them grew weary.

For the first time in days, their fatigue won over. Not only had his battle worn him out, but they had paid the toll as well. Before falling asleep, Annie glanced over once more as Jack's mouth hung open and his heartbeat increased.

She tried desperately to keep her eyes open, but the lack of sleep finally overtook her and her brothers as they gave in to their exhaustion and drifted into a much-needed slumber.

Moments later, startled by an odd clanking sound outside their room, Annie, Jack Jr., and Danny all awoke and immediately looked over to their father, Jack. With the lights dimmed, they struggled to grasp that something had changed.

They slowly rose and then rushed to his bedside. His breathing had ceased, and his increased heartbeat was nonexistent. They each kissed their father's cheek as the warmth of his skin remained. As they pulled away to gaze at him, something odd came over them.

They stared at him deeply and could not believe their eyes. His gaunt appearance and open-mouthed struggle had been wonderfully transformed. Instead, the three found themselves staring at their father, who had now gently closed his mouth in a smile of contentment.

Stunned at what they had experienced, Annie stepped away and said, "He's smiling. He's actually smiling."

"That's because he's with Mom," Danny said as all three of them hugged one another.

Instantaneously, Jack looked up, and he was back on the beach. He was now standing comfortably while happily resting in the arms of Jesus. Jesus looked at him and said, "Welcome home, Jack."

Still unsure of his environment, Jack looked around and saw Paraclete (the Holy Spirit) and God. Abisai and Michael stood on either side of him. God, Jesus, and the Holy Spirit all walked over to the books they had retrieved from the hut and placed them down on a new nightstand, which also held Jack's book.

Within seconds, the four books melded into one book with Jack's name prominently on it. Jesus went over, picked it up, and handed it to Jack. The book now featured only one page within its binding. Confused by the odd size, Jack took the book from Jesus and lifted the cover. As he did so, two blue butterflies fluttered out of the binding. Jack looked up as a red cardinal flew around him, and the palm trees swayed. He continued to open the book, and the only page inside featured the very familiar image of Dolly standing by the bar in Hawaii, holding the two mai tais. Underneath the image a caption read, "Turn around."

Surprised, Jack looked up at Jesus, who now had a smile on his face. He turned around and to his utter shock and sheer joy saw Dolly standing next to the bar holding the two mai tais. She was in the cute mango-colored top with white knee-high pants as the blue butterflies and a red cardinal fluttered in the wind around her.

"Oh my God. Dolly, it's you—it's really you!" he said in complete elation.

"Welcome home, honey!" Dolly said as she put the drinks down, and Jack ran toward her to absorb that familiar embrace he had been longing for, for years. As they hugged and kissed, Jack lost himself in the moment as he took in the warmest and most welcoming reunion he could have ever imagined.

After their lengthy embrace, Dolly looked at him with an amazing smile that could have lit up the universe and said, "Want to take a boat ride?"

Jack, who had a matching smile of utter joy, said, "Oh, I would love to take a boat ride with you!"

They both laughed as they kissed once more and turned toward a boat near the coastline. As they walked toward the boat, their only dog galloped up to them and joined them on their walk. They held hands as all three of them boarded the boat.

As they sailed, the most beautiful bright light appeared in the distance as they floated in its direction.

Soar is dedicated to
My Soulmate

CPSIA information can be obtained
at www.ICGtesting.com
Printed in the USA
BVHW052239221022
650079BV00005B/97

the setting. The flowers and the trees within the atrium complemented the various fountains and waterfalls sprinkled through the property.

As he followed the path, it took him to the center of the atrium which featured a large oval-shaped bar. Sitting at the bar holding a tropical drink was Michael. He waved to Jack as he took a sip of his cocktail.

Jack acknowledged Michael and walked up to him. "What are you drinking?" Michael asked as he pointed toward the bar.

Jack looked up and down the bar and said to the bartender nearby, "Um—hi, how ya doing? You know, I think I'll have an old-fashioned. It's been that kind of day."

"Old-fashioned coming up," the bartender said.

Michael moved slightly to allow for Jack to sit down next to him on a barstool. "This is quite a resort," Jack said.

"It's something, huh?" Michael replied.

"Old-fashioned," the bartender said as he placed Jack's drink on the bar.

"Wow, that was quick!" Jack said.

"Enjoy!" the bartender said as he wiped the counter near him and moved away from the two men.

Jack looked at the drink and settled into his barstool. He took a deep breath and sipped the drink. Then he looked over to Michael. "Can you please tell me what's going on here?"

Michael looked up from his drink and scanned the bar. "I believe it's happy hour."

Jack looked over cynically and said, "Come on. Where am I, Michael? What is going on with me?"

"I told you on the plane. You're going through transition," Michael replied.

"Transition? What's transition?" Jack asked.

"It's kind of like you're here, but you're not," Michael said. "Like a half-baked pie."

"A half-baked pie? That's what you're telling me? Is this Heaven? Am I dead?"

Michael started to laugh. "This? Is this Heaven? Oh no. Close, but not quite there yet."

"This is close? Man, this is a paradise," Jack said.

"You should see Heaven," Michael said.

Jack looked at Michael with concern and said, "Will I?"

"Just let the process work through. You will see," Michael assured him.

"I don't understand. What is the process? What do I have to do?" Jack asked.

"You really don't have to do anything," Michael replied. "I mean, most of it you have already done."

"I've done most of what? What do you mean?"

"It'll all come out. Don't you worry. How's your drink?"

"My drink? My drink is fine, but wait a second," Jack said, his concern rising. "How should I not worry? What have I done? Did I do something wrong? Am I in jeopardy?"

"*Jeopardy!*—oh, that really is a great show," Michael said. "As for you, no jeopardy, just a little talking."

"Talking about what?" Jack said.

"Well, we can start with you."

"Me?"

"Yeah, tell me something I should know about you," Michael said.

"I don't know. I mean, like what?"

"What motivates you? What keeps you going?"

"What motivates me? Ha!" Jack said sarcastically.

"Why do you laugh?"